Intrigue

MW00416250

"How do I know you're telling me the truth?"

He stared down at her. She was so close. All John would have to do was lean down just a bit more and he could taste the mouth he had fantasized about all day.

"You don't know," he answered in a voice so low Lana was forced to lean closer. "But if you're the reporter I think you are, you'll check out the facts before you write the story."

"I will check it out, you know," she whispered, trying to swallow the almost strangling lump of emotions that seemed to block her throat.

"I know that."

"I have to follow this lead." Lana watched his face move closer and she closed her eyes in anticipation.

"Yes, and I have to follow this lead." He closed the gap between them, pressing his lips against hers....

## ABOUT THE AUTHOR

Andrea Davidson began her writing career
with the American Medical Association in
Chicago and then wrote on a free-lance basis
after the birth of her first child. She is a
seasoned romance writer and now resides in
Houston, Texas.

## Books by Andrea Davidson

HARLEQUIN AMERICAN ROMANCES
16-MUSIC IN THE NIGHT
21-UNTAMED POSSESSION
45-TREASURES OF THE HEART

These books may be available at your local bookseller.

For a free catalog listing all titles currently available, send
your name and address to:

Harlequin Reader Service
P.O. Box 52040, Phoenix, AZ 85072-2040
Canadian address: Stratford, Ontario  N5A 6W2

# Treasures
# of the Heart

## ANDREA DAVIDSON

*Harlequin Books*

TORONTO • NEW YORK • LONDON
AMSTERDAM • PARIS • SYDNEY • HAMBURG
STOCKHOLM • ATHENS • TOKYO • MILAN

To my parents—
For introducing me to a land so rich with history,
it still echoes with the dreams of the past.

Published March 1984

ISBN 0-373-16045-3

Printed in Canada

"Where the wind was blowing across a high place...where the air was thin and full of silver sounds, and coyotes with bright yellow eyes...I smelled owls and sagebrush and small wild things. The whole universe was alive, vibrating all around that high windy place, and there was no more fear, because my father lives here."

—Tombstone epitaph
(near Irwin Lake, Colorado)

# *Chapter One*

So remote was it, that only the keen eye of the eagle soaring above it all with wide-spread wings could catch a glimpse of the rustic pine lodge in which John Ryan sat meditating. He sat alone in a brooding mood that flattened the normally handsome, intelligent features of his face. A glass of bourbon was held loosely between his fingers, but his grip tightened noticeably with each frown that pulled the corners of his mouth downward. John Ryan was strangely pensive today because he had finally come to accept the truth about the life he'd been building for fifteen years. It wasn't worth a damn.

He was sitting in the lodge bar, furnished in authentic 1890's decor, at a small wooden table located strategically in front of the large window overlooking the world below and beyond. The french doors were open at one end of the room and the late afternoon breeze lifted and held, then fell again in a rhythmic pattern of breathing.

John stared at a group of people sitting on the sun-warmed deck, sipping delicately at their Perriers and Chablis, their light banter carried by the wind into the open lodge, and he wondered if any of them were really happy. Deciding that they probably were not, he turned his attention back to the scenery.

Camouflaged so well by its sheltering canopy of trees, the lodge was nestled securely below a high, windy peak whose craggy face had been swept clean of trees by the constant driving force of wind and snow and time; where any plant or animal that dared to exist that high maintained its precarious hold on life by sheer determination alone.

It was a region cut by rivers and avalanches, scarred and gouged by abandoned and long-forgotten mines, a towering landscape sculptured lovingly by the hand of God.

Almost totally inaccessible except to its well-heeled guests, the lodge sat comfortably in the lap of the mountains, pressing itself into the soft bosom of gently rising slopes covered in Douglas fir and Englemann spruce.

It was wreathed on the back side by a necklace of pale green aspen; the front was walled with floor-to-ceiling windows that gazed down over a narrow valley of paintbrush, primrose, columbine, and a thousand other varieties of Alpine wildflowers. Beyond the valley were rising crests, and beyond that were more pinnacles, a seemingly endless rise and fall in the spine of Colorado's Rocky Mountain chain.

In the center of the narrow valley was a misty green lake, the trapped remnant of the Pleistocene glacial epoch that gave name to the remote mountain retreat known as Pine Lake Lodge.

Its owner, Dan Granger, weathered and venerable as a legendary pine, sat on a stool at the end of the bar wearing one of his faded flannel shirts. His left arm had been lost as a casualty of "the Big One," World War II. But, like a full-branched evergreen that has been pruned and gnarled by the forces of nature yet still stands tall, Dan thrived and grew hardier because of his adversity.

He was the only one who noticed the troubled glaze in John Ryan's eyes. He was the only one here who would make it his business to notice. After all, as owner of the lodge he wanted to know what made his guests happy, sad, mad, or any gradation of emotion in between.

The lodge had been conceived several years before as a rough-hewn Shangri-La, an isolated retreat for the adventuresome rich—those who came for a unique taste of rustic posh and those who liked the simple anonymity of it. He knew from the beginning he would have to keep the prices exorbitantly high in order to attract the quieter, wealthy clientele he wanted, and to keep out the less fortunate couples with slews of noisy children who wanted nothing more out of a vacation than video movies and electronic games to amuse them.

His guests—and he thought of them all as personal friends—were treated royally. The well-paid staff catered to their every need, knew the names of those who returned time and time again, and committed to heart their smallest likes or dislikes.

At sixty-three, Dan Granger was too wise to be a snob, but he was a man who liked his privacy. And he loved his guests. Especially this man sitting by the window with the weight of the world pressing down on his shoulders. Dan had been a friend of the Ryan family for longer than he could remember, and he had contributed substantially to John's campaign funds. If Dan's wife had been with him longer, and if they had been blessed with a son of their own, he could think of none better than John Ryan.

Slipping off the stool, he sauntered over toward the table, nodding a casual greeting now and then to the few patrons who were in the bar at this hour.

Dan sat down across from John and a waiter immediately appeared with a frosted mug of Coors for his boss.

"In another hour those trout will be biting."

Dan spoke to John without a formal greeting. There was no need. They had known each other too long for that.

The observation went unnoticed, but that too didn't matter.

A soft breath of air spilled into the room and the afternoon seemed to hang, suspended indefinitely, on that one fresh sigh.

An attractive young couple strolled arm in arm across the room and smiled intimately at one another. The young man reached around the girl with one hand, cupping her hip in an elemental invitation.

Dan and John watched the couple, then exchanged a silent look. "A marriage made in heaven," Dan said with a smile.

John smirked and took a sip of his drink. "Wonder how long it'll take for that one to descend into Hell."

Dan looked closely at the younger man. "You're a cynical bastard, John Ryan."

John laughed easily, showing a genuine smile for the first time all day. "You're right." He leaned an elbow onto the table and lowered his voice. "It's just that ever since they checked in next door to me, I lie awake at night imagining their sexual acrobatics on the other side of the wall." He shook his head and expelled a tight breath. "Frankly, I'm just sick and tired of thinking about those two."

Dan chuckled deeply. "Well, at least that's a sign that you're still among the living. I was beginning to wonder there for a while."

John's smile faded, replaced by a deepening frown. He stared gloomily into his glass of amber liquid then lifted his gaze to the scenery beyond the window. "What the hell am I doing here, Dan?"

"Resting."

John ignored the answer. "Do you know all that I have waiting for me on my desk in Washington? The budget committee is meeting tomorrow and I'm not going to be there. How will that look? What am I thinking about?"

"I would say that's the question, John. What are you thinking about? What's troubling you so?"

A long stretch of silence spanned between the two men.

"Is it Anne?" asked Dan.

"Anne." John spat the name out as if it had a foul taste. "Anne isn't worth thinking about. Never was."

"You were married to her for fifteen years."

"Married," John scoffed. "Is that what it was?"

Dan leaned back in his chair and rested his right forearm on the table. He turned his eyes toward the window, surveying the land around him. He owned a substantial portion of it, but he didn't think of it as his. It belonged to no one except perhaps to the mule deer, the big horn sheep, and the occasional mountain lion that traversed it in search of food and water. People came and went, taking bits and pieces of its substance home inside of them, but no one could ever really call it his own.

"You know, people come here for a lot of different reasons, John. And I can usually figure out what those reasons are, but this time... with you... I'm at a loss. He paused for effect. "What is it with you, John? What has you running scared?"

John looked at his friend for a long moment and sighed. "I wish I knew, Dan. I wish to hell I knew."

What more could he say? He had just turned forty and somehow, somewhere along the way, he had lost the clarity and direction in his life. That was something that was not easy to define. Even to old friends. He had been here for almost a week and the answers to his still vague questions had not yet come. He wondered if they ever would.

Lana ran her fingers through her shoulder-length, curly brown hair, trying to give it some semblance of control. With her lower lip protruded, she blew a few wavy tendrils out of her eyes. She shifted her purse to the opposite shoulder as she threaded her way through the lobby of the *Rocky Mountain*

*News* office building in downtown Denver. The weight of her tape recorder, notepads, and pens pulled the leather bag until it was cutting into the flesh of her shoulder.

She glanced at her watch again. Damn, she would have to hurry. She couldn't take a chance on missing Chuck. Her chance. Her pulse accelerated with the thought. This was her big chance. A shiver of excitement rippled down her spine, and a nonsensical ditty began to play through her head. *Puuulitzer Prize, Puuulitzer Priiize.* She smiled to herself and crossed the busy street, sidestepping the oncoming traffic with a buoyant stride.

She gazed up at the goldleaf dome of the state capitol just ahead and quickened her step. Nervously checking her watch again, she went over the meeting instructions Chuck had given her on the phone. He would be in the park, across from the capitol at twelve o'clock sharp, near the columns of that monstrous thing that looked like some Greco-Roman ruin. He had made it clear that he wasn't going to wait around. If she were late, then that was her tough luck.

By the time she reached the park, Lana was running, and the bag banged painfully against her hip until she was sure she would be bruised. She spotted him on the bench where he said he'd be, looking natty as always, yet as devoid of personality as nearly every other aide-de-camp at the state capitol.

Lana sat down beside him, holding her purse next to her chest while she gasped for breath. "Made it," she panted, waiting for her pulse rate to return to normal before she said anything else.

"You really get off on this cloak and dagger stuff, don't you, Munsinger?"

Lana looked long and hard at Chuck, frowning at his inability to understand. How could she make anyone see what this job meant to her, or make them understand the driving need she had to be all that her ancestral background demanded?

"I do what I have to do to get a story," she answered for lack of a better explanation. "Now, do you have something for me?"

He glanced around nervously as if they might be under serveillance. "I could get in a lot of trouble for this, you know."

"Look, Chuck, be reasonable. Who's going to find out? I'm certainly not going to tell."

Chuck expelled an anxious breath of air. "All right, Lana, but you owe me one."

She sighed impatiently. "Sure, Chuck. Sure."

"The governor had a conference call last week with our illustrious senators in Washington. And of course I was on another line taking notes and doing my secretarial duty."

"Do I detect a note of discontent with your job in there somewhere?"

"No comment," Chuck grumbled. "Anyway, after they finished their little long-distance powwow, Senator Jones hung up, but the governor asked Ryan to stay on. He obviously had forgotten that I was still on there, because they began discussing some highly confidential matters.''

"What were they talking about?" Lana had her notebook out and was already making shorthand notations on the paper.

"I can't talk about some of it. But I did hear them mention Abscam. The governor brought it up and our friend Ryan was upset that anyone knew about his involvement in it. Very upset."

"How could you tell? What did he say?"

"It wasn't what he said. It was the tone of voice. I swear I could hear the sweat dripping off his face on the other end of the line."

Lana's mouth turned down in irritation and she again sighed. "That's not much to go on, Chuck. A tone of voice? Big deal. Where's this tantalizing tidbit of information you have for me?"

Chuck leaned back lazily into the park bench, his mouth pulled sideways in a superior slash. He looked up through the trees above them with cocky self-assurance. "I know where he is."

"You're kidding." She narrowed her eyes on Chuck with a threat of slow torture if he were lying to her.

"Nope."

She shook her head in disbelief. "Some of the best reporters in the business have been trying to get hold of him for a week and nobody in his office will breathe even a clue."

Chuck smiled wickedly. "Now, tell me how wonderful I am, Lana. How you wouldn't have a story if it weren't for me."

"Tell me where he is first."

His mouth curved into a canary-eating grin. "At Pine Lake Lodge, holed up like a scared jack rabbit."

Lana stared blankly at the young man for several long seconds, then shrugged. "Okay, Chuck, I give up. Where the hell is Pine Lake Lodge?"

"Where the hell is Pine Lake Lodge?" the city editor bellowed. Even though Lana was only two feet away, Walter Finch wouldn't know how not to bellow if his life depended upon it.

Lana pulled out her map of Colorado and laid it across his desk, flattening the creases with her palms. "Look, right in here ... somewhere."

Walter Finch looked at the slim, insistent woman beside him. She had such eager green eyes, eyes that missed nothing, that seemed to see everything and yet allowed others very few glimpses of the woman inside. He shook his head over her determination. "That's a little vague, isn't it? You're going to have to pin it down to something more specific than between Gunnison and Aspen. You're talking about a lot of acreage."

"Well, it's around this area ... I think. Up Schofield Pass. Probably right here."

"Lana, you're talking about some of the most
remote territory in this country. How come I've
never heard of this place? And who told you the
senator was there?"

"A source."

"What source?"

"A reliable one, Walt. You're going to have to
trust me on this one. I think I've really got something here."

"What happened to that story you promised me
yesterday—the one on the retirement home crafts
fair? Huh? Huh?"

Lana waved her hand distractedly. She began
counting off the essential considerations on her
fingers. "First, a high ranking source in the state
capitol slipped the information when I was talking
to him yesterday. Senator Ryan was involved in
Abscam, Walter. And, they are hiding that information."

"Abscam was four years ago, Lana. Old news."

Lana ignored his argument as she continued to
defend her case. "Second, the senator was never
charged with anything. His name was never even
released to the press, and when I called the F.B.I.
they refused to talk about it. Now I ask you why?"

Walter Finch opened his mouth to comment,
but Lana rushed ahead with her own answer.

"Because of his family's influence, that's why.

Because they hold title to some of this country's most valuable land. Coal, Walter." Her face tightened with the gravity of her own words. "Coal, molybdenum, uranium, copper—"

"I get the picture, Lana." Walt was rapidly tiring of this conversation. They were on deadline and he had too many other things to think about right now. What was he going to do with this woman? She tried so hard. Too hard most of the time. And she never knew when to stop pushing. For some reason, that kind of intensity and self-imposed pressure in a reporter made him nervous.

"Okay," she continued. "So now, other high-ranking government officials have gotten wind of it and here's Ryan hiding out in the mountains until the foul stench all blows over."

Lana became more fervent when she sensed skepticism—or was it just plain lack of interest— radiating from the city editor's eyes even though he never moved a muscle. "Look, Walt, the guy's a hopeful for the presidential nod in a few years. This is big news. I really think I'm on to something."

Walt tapped his pencil on the desk and stared at Lana for so long she thought she would scream.

"I want to hear from you every day, Munsinger. Every day. Do you understand me?" The pencil was now pointed at her in deadly warning, but she didn't notice.

She was ecstatic. Her editor had given her the green light. She was going to Pine Lake—wherever on God's green earth that was—and she was going to get a story. A real story for a change. And, in the process, she would bring down that right-wing Tory, John Ryan, and all of the conservative, dyed-in-the-wool policies he clung to so vehemently. Oh, what a glorious day this was!

As the day wore on, it turned out to be somewhat less than glorious. The owner of Pine Lake Lodge was not exactly thrilled with the prospect of a journalist coming to stay, and Lana had to use all of her powers of persuasion, mixed with a fair amount of doubletalk, to convince the man that she was harmless. He made it very clear that he did not want his establishment to appear in the pages of any—he repeated several times—travel magazine. Lana had to assure him that she was there only to do research on her family's background, and even then the man was skeptical. But he did finally accept her reservation on short notice.

The second snag in her plans came from Walt. "They charge how much a night!" The thunder of his voice rolled across the newsroom floor.

Lana cringed. "Walt, think of it as an investment. Think of the story I'm going to get out of this. The story this paper is going to get."

"It had better be one hell of a return on that investment, Munsinger, or your neck is going on the chopping block. Do I make myself clear?"

"Aye, aye, Captain." Lana saluted and quickly walked back to her desk to gather up her recorder and purse. Walter Finch watched her with narrowed eyes, trying to decide whether her remark and gesture had been insubordinate or not. Grumbling incoherently, he picked up the phone and was soon bellowing into someone else's ear.

The sky was a lazy, cloudless blue and a warm summer breeze was blowing down from the mountains as Lana drove the next morning from Denver to Crested Butte. The trip took about five and a half hours, but she didn't mind. It was the first really free morning she'd had in a long time. Every waking moment, it seemed, was spent on either researching a story and gathering facts, interviewing and writing the copy, or typing it up into final form. This five-hour stretch was a welcomed relief. Besides, she needed this quiet time to plan her strategy. This was one story she didn't want to louse up. It was just too damn important.

She had been waiting for her break for so many years; all her life, or so it seemed. Everyone else had been waiting for it too. Expecting and waiting. Wondering silently why it hadn't yet come. She could see it in everyone's eyes. She knew what they expected of her. This curse had been genetically implanted within her a long time ago and it wasn't about to go away. She had to fulfill her destiny.

In 1881 her great-grandfather, Samuel Munsinger, had traveled from Denver to Gunnison County, Colorado, all in the line of duty. A respected reporter for the *Denver Republican*, he was working on a story about some of the more infamous mining towns in western Colorado: Tin Cup, Taylor Park, Gothic, and Irwin. Locations that conjure up a vision of hardy, never-say-die men who, hearing tales of enough gold and silver to make a man rich beyond his wildest dreams, forged their way into the remote mountains like flies in search of honey. A land filled with a rich array of colorful characters like Alfred Packer "the Colorado Maneater," Ham Bone Jane, and Timberline Kate, so called because of her receding hairline.

A whole new pattern of life developed within that harsh and unyielding land in the late nineteenth century, and Samuel Munsinger wanted to recount it. But before he could finish the story he was killed in Pearl Pass by a renegade band of Ute Indians, angry over their removal to the new Uintah Reservation in Utah.

His untimely and rather sensational death made him a kind of legend or folk hero in Colorado's dynamic history. His incurably inquisitive nose for a story and his stubborn perserverance in following a lead had also been carried down through the blood and genes of Lana's grandfather, Frederick, then her father, and finally trickling down to her.

Frederick Munsinger had followed his adventurous father's footsteps up into the mountains, settling finally in Crested Butte where he had been editor of the *Weekly Citizen* for thirty years.

Lana's father, Samuel, had moved back into the folds of city life, establishing himself as one of the most highly respected journalists in the United States. While maintaining residence in Denver, his articles were read in every paper from New York to Oregon, and he received distinguished awards from the New York *Times*, the New York *Herald Tribune*, the Chicago *Daily News*, and the *Washington Post*.

With a family tree as resplendent with notable achievements as Lana's was, it was no wonder the world—or at least the world of journalism—was waiting for the old Munsinger magic to shine through.

For five years Lana had been striving for that same recognition and status, and for five long years she had watched all of the best stories go to someone else. None of the editors seemed to understand how badly she needed a good story. She had to do it! It was expected of her.

She was sure, if the statistics were made available, that she had covered more cute zoo stories, more dull city council meeings, more tedious boat shows and uninspired arts and crafts festivals than anyone in the history of journalism.

But now, now she had a real story. Finally. One with lots of meat into which she could sink her teeth. What could be better than a political scandal in the career of one of the country's most influential men, a man who was no doubt going to run for president in a few years, a man whose marriage had been plagued with ugly rumors and innuendos for years, and a man whose political beliefs ran a hundred and eighty degrees opposite of Lana's? It was the story of a lifetime. A chance to bring down one of the scions of the Ryan empire. An opportunity to fulfill her destiny. A chance to show the world that she had the same Munsinger magic the rest of her family had.

*Pulitzer Prize, Lana. This time you're really going to do it. John Ryan's political demise is going to be your banner headline to fame and fortune.*

It never entered her very determined mind that John Ryan might have something to say about that. All she knew was that she had to do this—had to—and nothing was going to get in her way.

# Chapter Two

The afternoon breeze that blew through the open window of the truck was warm against her face. But it had the distinct smell of pine, a clean fresh fragrance that cut right through the dense layers of oppressive city air.

"What kind of a nut would build a resort up here?"

The driver smiled at her candor. Marve had picked her up in Crested Butte where she had parked her Subaru. He was used to the guests at the lodge. You could learn a lot about human nature and about people just driving them back and forth.

"You aren't by any chance related to the owner, are you?"

"No."

"Oh good," she sighed, vastly relieved. As a journalist, Lana had seen all kinds of eccentricities, but nothing had prepared her for this. What kind of an oddball would build a hotel in the middle of nowhere?

"How long will you be staying at the lodge?" Marve turned the wheel sharply to avoid a large boulder in the road.

"I don't know. I'm going to be doing some... research." Lana turned her head toward the window so the man could not read her expression. "So...."

"In other words, it all depends on when you get what you want, right?"

"Exactly."

They drove along the treacherous shelf road above Emerald Lake, through Schofield Pass and into the Elk Mountains and Marve pointed out various sights of interest and related some of the history of the area. Quaint and picturesque names like Rustler's Gulch, Oh-Be-Joyful Creek, and Fabulous Valley rolled easily from his mouth.

This was a land so violent, fur trappers in the early nineteenth century virtually ignored it; so formidable that railroads skirted it rather than fail at conquering it; so unyielding, the Ute Indians had to winter elsewhere. And yet, here in this harsh land, a man had built an outrageously expensive resort for the rich and famous. Lana shook her head again.

As the four-wheel drive jeep conquered the last seemingly insurmountable rise, the lodge came into view. Lana's first reaction was one of stunned disbelief. Surrounded by towering mountains, the valley was totally isolated from the outside world. Sharp rock ridges intersected lush green slopes, and stands of pine trees hovered in dark privacy around the lodge.

Driving to the far end of the lake, the jeep forded a shallow pool, jets of water spraying up and out from the wheels. As they climbed the last gentle hill, Lana got her first good look at the lodge.

Basically a large rectangle built of hand-notched logs, it was looped by a large cedar deck that afforded a relaxing view of the scenery from any side of the hotel. Several guests were already taking advantage of the early afternoon sun, their feet propped up on extra chairs, tall cool drinks in their hands. Racks for skis, unused at this time of the year, were bolted to the outside walls. A large stone chimney rose from the center of the structure, and smaller ones protruded from the roof at regular intervals. Lana could also see that each room had its own small, but very private, deck.

"Well, here we are," the driver unnecessarily pointed out. "Ready?"

Lana looked around at the towering mountains that surrounded the lodge, at the expanse of utter wilderness that lay between her and her car back in Crested Butte. A lot depended on this story. Her self-esteem, her editor's praise, her father's pride. "No," she finally answered. "I'm not sure that I am ready."

The driver chuckled as they both climbed from the jeep and he reached for her suitcase in the back seat. "You're going to love it here, Miss

Munsinger. You'll never want to leave. This place will keep you young."

"Sounds too much like Shangri-La for my tastes."

"Exactly!" a different voice boomed beside her.

Lana spun around to face the large, rugged man who had addressed her. "You must be Lana Munsinger. I'm Dan Granger. Welcome to Pine Lake Lodge." He extended his hand and she was almost overwhelmed by the size and strength of it. Her eyes jumped to the left sleeve of his red flannel shirt, which was tucked neatly into the waistband of his jeans, then quickly shifted back to his face, holding at bay any surprise she might have felt. His hair was sprinkled with ashen gray and his skin was the texture of fine bronzed leather.

"I hope the trip up here wasn't too taxing." His smile was that of the perfect host.

"No, it was breathtaking. Actually I was so involved with the scenery that time slipped away from me."

Dan laughed and the sound of it was rich and full-bodied like the man. "That's what happens to you up here in these mountains. It takes hold of you somehow." He was gazing off across the valley and Lana followed his line of vision. The aspen leaves quivered in the afternoon light and the lake basked tranquilly in the glow of the sun. The mountains surrounding it were so steep and the valley so narrow that the lake would be in full sun for only about three or four hours a day.

"Well, are you ready for a tour of my humble abode?" Dan placed his arm around Lana's shoulders and began leading her up the stairs of the deck. There was nothing brash in the gesture at all and to Lana it seemed the most natural thing in the world. The man was already a friend.

"Humble abode?" Her laugh was skeptical. "At these prices, how can it or you remain humble?"

Dan looked at her appreciatively. "A lady who speaks her mind." He nodded. "I think this place is going to suit you, Miss Munsinger." He held open the large wooden front door for her and waited for her to enter. A small slip of a woman, young, attractive, middle class. Interesting eyes. Not at all what he'd expected.

"I hope it suits me," she mumbled. It had better suit her well enough to give her a story or her editor would probably pack her in a suit of cement and drop her in the South Platte River.

She paused before entering the lodge, and an ominous chill slid down her neck and back as she noticed a small plaque above the door that warned, "There are strange things done, in the midnight sun, by the men who moil for gold."

She looked up at Dan and smiled shakily. "Interesting."

"Yes, isn't it?" he answered vaguely. "Well, what do you think?" He swept his arm about the room, apparently oblivious of her sudden attack of nerves.

Almost the entire lower floor of the lodge was one open area. The center arcade was floored in pine while on each side were small, carpeted conversation areas. In the center of the room was a huge, copper-hooded circular fireplace, and at each end of the building were sweeping Y-shaped staircases that led to the upper balconies where the guests' rooms were. On the far wall hung a magnificent fur of a Kodiak, and all around the large room hung memorabilia from the early mining days.

"Unbelievable!" Lana turned slowly to have a full view of the entire first floor. "I'm impressed, Mr. Granger. Did you design this all by yourself?"

"I designed the exterior and my wife did all the interior decorating." His face glowed with pride over the creation.

"I hope I'll be able to meet her and tell her what a fantastic job she did."

"I wish you could, but she passed away four years ago." A flicker of sadness darted across the man's eyes and Lana felt a tremor of unhappiness from her own past shudder through her. Funny how she could still be affected so, even by the mention of a stranger's death. She pushed the feeling away. Painful memories were best left in the past where they belonged.

"I'm sorry."

"So am I. She was a very special woman." He shrugged. "But we all learn to adjust and I have to admit, this place has a curative effect on most people. Even on someone as ornery as I am. Now then"—Dan slapped his hand against his rock hard stomach, signaling an end to the conversation about his personal life—"about you. What kinds of things are you interested in doing while you're here?"

Lana pulled the story she had rehearsed to the front of her mind. "Well, I wanted to visit some of the old mining sites. My great-grandfather did some reporting up here during the late nineteenth century."

Dan pursed his lips. "Yes, I know. Samuel Munsinger." Noticing Lana's surprise, he explained. "Call me nosy if you will, Miss Munsinger. But I make it a habit to know who my guests are. And your grandfather and great-grandfather were well known in these parts."

Lana felt a temporary tremor of doubt course through her veins. How much did he find out? How much does he know about her and about what she is doing here? "Well," she laughed somewhat uneasily. "Now you know why I'm so interested in learning more about them. I never took the time before and ...." Another giggle escaped. "So anyway, here I am."

"Yes, here you are." Dan watched her carefully

and knew, somehow, that this woman was not telling the whole truth. Her eyes were very revealing, and yet it was difficult to know exactly what it was that you were seeing in them. He would have to keep an eye on her. A very careful eye. "Come on, I'll show you your room."

"Do you do this for all your guests, Mr. Granger?"

"What's that?"

"This special treatment. I feel like the red carpet has been rolled out for me."

"Just part of the service here. We aim to please. I do hope that if there's anything you want, anything at all, you'll let me or anyone on the staff know. We'll be glad to provide you with whatever you need."

"Thank you, I'll remember that." Lana smiled, trying to keep the awe out of her voice. "Don't I need to register at the desk first?"

"No, that's all been taken care of. The idea here is to relax and let us take care of you. Sound good?"

"Sounds fantastic. Although I might become so spoiled, I won't want to leave."

"Dan!" A voice behind them cried out. "I saw them! I finally saw them!" They were attempting to climb the wide staircase at one end of the lobby, when the deep, excited voice halted their progress.

They stopped and turned. John Ryan took the

stairs two at a time until he was even with them. He smiled politely at Lana, but his attention was obviously on another track. "Sorry to bother you, Dan. Just thought you'd like to know. I finally saw them." He was grinning from ear to ear and Dan knew immediately what he was talking about.

"You look like a man who has just seen a corner of heaven."

"I have. Beautiful!"

Lana was thoroughly confused, but neither man seemed inclined to include her in the conversation. She had been watching Ryan closely ever since he bounded up the stairs like an eager puppy, getting a general impression of the man from a distance before confronting him. It would give her the advantage, knowing all about him before he knew anything about her. She already knew what he looked like. His face had been smeared across the papers and television screen more times than she cared to remember.

But she was surprised at how different he looked in person. They say photographs never lie. But if this was John Ryan, who was the man in the papers? His dark brown hair was windblown, a stark contradiction to the immaculately styled public image he cultivated. He was wearing a plaid cowboy shirt with pearl snaps down the front, faded blue jeans, and brown leather boots. In every photograph she had seen, and in the press conferences of his that she had attended, he'd looked like a department store mannequin wearing nothing but conservative three-piece suits.

But when he finally turned to face her, every preconceived notion, every previous image of him flew right out the window. There was something so blatantly sexual about the man that she could only stare. Something virile yet understated, bold yet defenseless. Her one fleeting moment of sanity had her wondering if her mouth was hanging open.

His spice brown eyes zeroed in on her, narrowing as if trying to place her face among the montage of faces he had met in his years as a politician. They were quiet eyes, she noticed, a little too serious perhaps, but thoughtful. He would not be a man to speak without thinking first. He had elegant features, not perfect but noble somehow and refined. He held out his hand to her and smiled, but before he could speak again, Dan was introducing them.

"Lana, let me introduce John Ryan. John, this is Lana Munsinger."

Their hands met and held for only a brief moment. But something about his touch activated the summer-rich juices in her body. And by the warm electric current that passed from his eyes to hers, she knew the sensation was mutual.

He stared at her for several long seconds. She was a beautiful woman. Very unusual looking with those green almond eyes and that mass of curly hair that hung below her shoulders. Maybe she was one of those empty-headed females who spent endless hours in hot rollers. But no, she really didn't look the type. And from what he could tell with the loose blouse and slacks she was wearing, she had a great body. Nice soft curves that would feel good under the stroke of a hand.

His eyes narrowed again. Now that he thought about it, there was something vaguely familiar about her. He was almost sure he had seen her somewhere before. But where? He glanced at Dan for elaboration.

As if on cue, Dan filled in the missing pieces. "Lana is a journalist from Denver. The *Rocky Mountain News*, isn't it Lana?"

"Yes." She hadn't failed to notice a hint of something in Dan's voice when he told John she was a journalist. Was it warning? A watch-out-she's-one-of-those-snoopy-reporter-types? Whatever it was, she was aware immediately of the change in John's eyes. Where only a moment before, they had been warmly aglow, now they appeared glazed, protected, even a little insecure.

Whether his inflections and tone had been intentional or not, Dan continued without missing a beat. "John has been out hiking this morning and he has finally seen the herd of big horn sheep that graze in this area. I've been telling him it was something he had to see before he left here."

"Oh?" Lana shot for nonchalance. "And when will that be?"

John focused on her eyes, then her mouth, then the tight set of her jaw. This was no idle question, no polite social repartee. This was interrogation time. He was sure he had seen her look that way before. Maybe at a press conference in Denver? Somewhere. Somewhere he had seen her and that look. Why was she here? Ever since he found out that the governor knew about his involvement in Abscam, he had become media skittish. He knew it was absurd to think that this woman knew anything. Still, he didn't want any over eager reporter on his trail the whole time he was up here.

"A little while longer," he answered vaguely, but he couldn't seem to tear his eyes away from her. After a too long, embarrassing stare, he forcefully switched his gaze to Dan. "Sorry I interrupted. I won't keep you any longer. See you later, Dan." He nodded at Lana without looking at her. "Nice meeting you, Miss Munsinger."

"Sen—Mr. Ryan." She flashed a nervous, but engaging smile, hoping he hadn't caught her slip of the tongue.

He had. And his eyes narrowed on her once again. He had heard her correctly. She had started to call him Senator. Dan hadn't mentioned that he was a senator. This woman knew. And, for some reason, she didn't want him to know she knew.

He tried to smile as he turned to walk away, but she caught a flicker of vulnerability, a loose thread of worry in his eyes before he turned.

Dan watched Lana watching John as he walked down the stairway and he wondered again what she was doing here. "I forgot to point out the restaurant and bar when we were downstairs," he said, making another mental note to keep an eye on this lady. "They're right through that doorway behind the staircase. Oh, by the way, what's your favorite drink?"

"Frozen margarita," she answered distractedly, her thoughts still honed in on the man she had just met. "Why?"

They had reached the upper floor and were walking down the landing toward her room. "Our bartender always wants to know. If a guest likes something very exotic, he wants to make sure he has the right ingredients. Here we are, number eighteen." Extracting a key from his right pocket, he opened the door and gestured for Lana to enter.

The room was as charming as the rest of the lodge, rustic but still luxurious. Almost austere in its simplicity, it had a fresh-scrubbed, down-home warmth in its decor. From the four-poster bed to the snuggly down quilts, the wooden nightstand with a crock full of fresh-cut flowers on top of it to the pine settee with its soft quilted pad, the old world charm poured forth. Duck decoys, candles in wooden candlesticks, and turn-of-the-century memorabilia added a homespun texture. A small stone fireplace filled one corner and a drop leaf table was placed against another wall.

"I am definitely never going to leave," Lana said with a laugh as she walked around the room. Even the bathroom was equipped with every modern convenience while still maintaining the historic flavor. The clawfoot tub was painted an amber enamel and on the wall above it was a large mantel mirror complete with a perched angel. Plants in baskets and a tin can filled with dried herbs sat on one shelf, while below it were several bottles of bath oils, cotton balls, and perfumes.

"I think I've died and gone to heaven. This is unbelievable!" She stared at Dan with open admiration. "I have to admit, I've never been anyplace like this before."

"Glad you like it, Lana. I'm going to leave you alone now. If you want someone to unpack your suitcase for you, just push this button." He pointed to one on the wall by the door. "If you need anything in fact, just push it. I'll see you later probably in the bar or at dinner. Make yourself at home and remember, if you need anything . . . ."

"I'll push the button." She laughed. "Thank you, Mr. Granger."

"We're pretty informal around here, so I insist you call me Dan."

"Okay, Dan."

Dan pulled the door closed behind him and

Lana was left alone. She walked around the room slowly, somewhat hesitantly, touching everything, trying to absorb the ambience, yet unable to believe that she was actually here. She opened the simple white curtains that covered the french doors to her balcony, and here another surprise awaited her. A small, round cedar hottub dominated one half of the balcony. The sides of her private deck were walled with pine slats to afford privacy from the other rooms, but the front view was left open to the spendor of the valley and lake below.

She stood still, gazing out over the valley until a knock on the door broke the hypnotic spell she was under. She walked to the door and opened it to a young man in a rust-colored Pine Lake Lodge jacket. He held out a frozen margarita to her. "All of the staff hopes you enjoy your stay, Miss Munsinger," he smiled, again with that perfect solicitous curve of lips, and Lana shook her head in wonder.

"Thank you," she answered, hoping her voice didn't sound as out-of-place as she felt. Closing the door once again, she set the glass on the bedside table and dropped to the bed, hugging a calico pillow to her mouth to stifle her uncustomary squeal of delight. "If Walter Finch could see me now! Now I know why this place is so damn expensive."

She propped up against her pillows, kicked off her shoes, and sipped leisurely on the delicious drink. It would be very easy to forget why she was here. The man she just met in the hallway would make it even easier. John Ryan. Lana shook her head in bemusement. He certainly didn't present the image she had expected. He seemed so approachable in his jeans and western shirt, his hairstyle obviously the least of his worries.

Her eyes closed involuntarily at the thought of his hand touching hers. *Oh, don't be a total idiot, Lana. You've touched a few men's hands in your lifetime. What's so different about this one?* She took a deep breath, letting it out slowly, deliberately. Something was different, that much she knew.

But, of course, it was just a physical fancy. Nothing more. It would go away. But her job, that's what was important. She was here for a very important assignment, and she wasn't going to screw it up over a trivial physical urge. She had a job to do, and she would do it. She rapped the bed with her fist for emphasis, then leaned back to sip on her drink, relieved that she had pulled out of her momentary lapse of duty.

But the image of the man—the new personal image—would not go away. She leaned against her pillow and thought for a long time about the man whose career she had come to crush. Not about the senator, but about the man. John Ryan.

John knocked the mud and grass off his boots before he walked up the steps of the deck. Still wearing his waterproof pants, and carrying his fishing boots, knapsack, and pole, he smiled to the waiter who congratulated him on his catch. "Thanks. I had to throw back three small ones, but looks like I've got a couple of keepers here. Would you have these cooked up for my dinner, please?"

"No problem at all, Senator Ryan. We'd be happy to do that."

John knew he didn't need to remind the waiter how he liked his trout fixed. The cook would remember it perfectly. Rolled in cornmeal, then baked to a golden brown with just a squeeze of lemon over them. His mouth was watering already over the thought of it.

He sat in a chair on the deck and began unstrapping the fishing pants from his jeans. Another waiter immediately appeared with a tall glass of iced tea. They all knew that after a day of fishing the senator preferred tea to alcohol.

On the other hand, Mrs. Rosenblum from New York liked lemonade in the afternoon, while Mrs. Fisch from Dallas always had a martini, very dry, and the newly-wedded Barkers wanted only champagne, Moet et Chandon 1959. It was a formidable task remembering every little fancy and whim of their guests, but the employees were paid extremely well for their faculties of recall. And they all knew from past experience that one little slip was all it took to be "retired" from the staff.

John sipped at the tea and relaxed in the midafternoon sun. He watched as Justine Moreau, the "queen of B movies," walked out onto the deck and plopped into a chair with her drink in her hand. Plopped was not exactly the way to describe such a voluptuous fanny, he decided. Jiggled or wiggled her more curvaceous assets into the chair was the best way to view it. And view it he did. She smiled none too coyly at John and he smiled back.

He took another sip of his drink while he watched her. She was even more gorgeous than she appeared on screen. And what male over the age of thirteen hadn't seen her latest film? Not much of an actress, to be sure. But then, who cared? Nobody went to see her films for the acting anyway.

She had been here at the lodge all week and John had been given more than enough encouragement to approach her. But for some reason he couldn't fathom, the prospect left him feeling hollow. It frightened him in a way. Maybe he had been married too long. Maybe Anne had done more permanent damage than he realized. He knew it was nothing physical. But emotional maybe.

Dan was right, he had become a cynical bastard when it came to male-female relationships. This way was better. A solitary man. No woman to drain you dry of every emotion.

He massaged a tight spot on his neck and drank

the last of his tea. A waiter immediately appeared to refill the glass, adding a few cubes of ice with the tongs and bucket that sat on top of his cart.

John closed his eyes, relishing all the luxury. Absolutely no responsibility! He knew it couldn't last much longer, but for now he was going to try and not think about Washington, Congress, the President's new budget plan, Anne's lawyers breathing down his neck, the latest oil crisis in the Mideast, or the hectic campaign schedule that would begin again in September.

It was all becoming such a drain. Definitely dried up. Where was the challenge? Everything he had ever wanted had always just been there, like juicy hors d'oeuvres on a platter, ready for him to pick and choose whatever he wanted. He had never had to work for anything.

In fact the only blemishes in his ten years of political life had been in regard to his wife and this Abscam mess in which he had reluctantly become involved. Thank God it never reached the press. His mind automatically flitted to the young woman he had met earlier this afternoon. Lana Munsinger. A sharp electrical impulse shot down through the center of his body, relieving him of any previous worries he'd had about his masculinity.

He expelled a quick breath. What was it about that particular woman that would have caused such a strong reaction? he wondered. He thought about her, remembering the vivid green eyes that had drilled deep inside of him, searching out every little facet of his personality. Eyes that seemed to see everything that was inside of him. And her mouth, soft and sensual. Her slight build. He wished now that he had examined her body more carefully. But how crude would that have been! As it was, it seemed that he'd stood there ogle-eyed like some sex-starved maniac.

And then to find out she was a reporter. Damn! It might be kind of nice to sit out on the deck and indulge in a few sexual fantasies about that woman, but not when she was a reporter. He'd had his fill of that breed in his professional life and he wanted absolutely nothing to do with it in his personal one.

But what was she doing here? Working on a story? And, if so, what kind? He certainly hoped she wouldn't decide to hound him now that she knew he was here. So far nothing had reached the press about this Abscam mess he was in. He wanted to make damn sure it stayed that way. Not that it would bother him personally. In fact, maybe it would spark things up a bit around the old campaign office, add a little fire or a bit of challenge. But the press coverage would kill his father. He was too old and sick to take any scandal in the family and John was thankful that he had been spared from hearing it.

He had to admit that that too was a drain. He

had been living a lie now for too long. Trying to please his constituents, his father, and the press at the same time. He had already come to the conclusion that, even if he lost the next election for the Senate, he would not be deeply upset. If he lost, then he wouldn't have to make the choice of whether he wanted to continue in politics or not. How simple it would be. He sighed. For some reason the idea suddenly seemed as desperate as setting fire to a factory when it no longer made a profit.

"You're a chicken, Ryan," he murmured into his glass. "A damn lily-livered fool."

Lana stood in the doorway of the bar, and watched John Ryan mumble into his drink.

She had been standing here watching him for several minutes, again getting an overall picture of who and what the man was. But there was an essence about him that disturbed her, tugging her in the wrong direction. There was something too solitary about him sitting on the deck of this remote lodge, talking into his drink. Something that didn't quite fit the mold.

She continued watching from the shadowy interior as a waiter brought a plate of small sandwiches to his table. *Okay, Lana, this is it. If you want a story, you'd better make your move.* She stood as straight and tall as her five foot six frame would allow and walked with a determined stride toward the man who was to be her ticket to fame.

John had picked up a wedged sandwich of chopped egg, tomato, and caviar and was just about to take a bite when Lana sat down. The sandwich stopped inches from his mouth as he stared at her.

"Hi." She smiled and reached for a sandwich as if they had been set there especially for her. "You don't mind, do you?"

John didn't take his eyes off her as he slowly bit into the sandwich. "Help yourself," he answered, his tone guarded and a little pungent. He tried not to stare at her as she licked a dab of egg off her fingers. But at the flick of that tongue, his blood began to bound against the surface of his skin, and he felt a light film of perspiration in the palms of his hands. Wiping them across his jeans nonchalantly, he tried to conjure up a feeling of annoyance at her for disturbing his solitude.

"I didn't think reporters took vacations, Miss Munsinger." John's eyes shifted to Dan Granger who had been watching the exchange from the door of the bar. As the two men's eyes locked, a moment of silent question and answer passed between them.

"It's Lana. Miss Munsinger sounds like an old grade school teacher. And I'm on assignment." She took another bite of sandwich and smiled at the waiter who immediately came over to the table. She looked over at John's glass. "Is that tea?"

"Yes," he answered stonily, hesitant even to let her know that much about him.

"I'll have the same." With the waiter dismissed, she turned back to John. "Listen, John— May I call you John?"

"You just did. Haven't I seen you at some press conferences before? Badgering and harassing me from the back row?"

She was looking at him directly now, straight into his solemn brown eyes, and she swallowed the clutching sensation of hesitancy that gripped her stomach. *Do not let this man affect you this way, Lana. Where is your objectivity? You are here to get your big story. And this man and his family are the epitome of greed and corruption in this country's political system. Bring him down, Lana. Bring him to his knees.*

Lana cleared her throat. "I'm going to come right to the point, John. I—"

Before she could say another word, Dan Granger picked up the chair next to John, turning it backwards and straddling it with his huge body. He rested his arm on the back of the chair and leaned toward it. "Well, Lana, I see you're settled in."

He smiled and sounded friendly enough, but Lana didn't fail to notice a hint of admonition in the deep bass voice. Dan turned to the younger man. "How was the fishing, John?"

"Great." He tried not to smile with too much relief over Dan's intervention.

"Tomorrow you let Marve drive you up the canyon a ways. The fishing's s'posed to be real good up the East Fork this time of year."

"Yeah, I may do that." John glanced at Lana with a sense of victory in his eyes. "Do you fish?"

Lana knew when she had been bamboozled and these two men had just done exactly that to her. They had outmaneuvered her with their innocent small talk and she wasn't going to get a chance to talk to John Ryan about anything more substantial than fishing or hiking. They were going to make sure of it. But she wasn't one to give up easily, especially when the reward was so high.

"Yes, I do. Maybe the two of us could—"

"I'm sure Dan here will be able to show you some great spots." John smiled the perfect candidate smile and she wanted to scream. This was not going to be an easy task getting this story, but she would just have to plan her strategy a little more carefully.

"Why don't you let me show you our stables, Lana. We've got some beautiful quarter horses." Dan was already standing and waiting for her to join him, so she had little choice in the matter.

*All right, you guys, you won this heat. I'll grant you that. But I'll catch up with you on the next.* "That will be fine, Dan." She smiled tightly at the two men, then stood to follow the owner of the lodge. They had walked about five feet away when Lana suddenly turned around and walked back to John.

Stopping directly in front of him, she cocked her head. "Would you like to have dinner tonight?"

John kept his hands flattened on the tops of his legs. She was standing in front of him, her torso within reach. All he'd have to do is lift his hands and rest them on her slim waist. But then he noticed the determined look in her eyes. Almost desperate. Just what the world needed, another desperate reporter. He had to give this one credit, she was dauntless. But if it were up to him, he'd ship every journalist he'd ever known off to Siberia. And this sexy little lady could lead the pack.

"I'd planned on having dinner, Miss Munsinger."

"I meant with me." She wasn't going to lose her temper. She wasn't... wasn't.

He chuckled, but the sound was devoid of amusement. "I'm kind of the old-fashioned type. I like to be the one to ask a lady out."

Lana observed him closely for a long moment. "And how long will I have to wait for you to ask me to dinner?"

The smile faded from his face as his eyes locked with hers. Of all the women in the world to have a sexual desire for, why did it have to be this one? He wasn't going to have anything to do with her. She was trouble, and he didn't want or need that right now. *Get her out your mind, John. Right now.* His gaze dropped to her mouth and then moved back to her eyes, and his voice was clear and determined. "Until hell freezes over."

Lana didn't even move for several seconds. Finally, pursing her lips in vexation, she turned and stalked off, catching up with Dan Granger, who had viewed the entire episode with a delighted gleam in his eyes.

John watched the sway of her body as she moved away. He couldn't take his eyes away from the tight fit of her corduroy pants over her hips. He forced himself to look away, to try and catch the attention of the bubble-headed bleached blond actress. But she was already engaged in an intimate tête-à-tête with a theatre critic from New York. It was just as well, John decided. He wasn't really interested anyway. In any woman. Especially some conniving, prying, green-eyed journalist with a delicious derriere.

The newly-wedded Barkers were seated two tables away and John grimaced with disgust. Why didn't they go fondle each other somewhere else? His eyes involuntarily shifted back to Lana Munsinger walking toward the stables with Dan and he wondered what kind of havoc she was going to wreak in his professional and personal life. Whatever kind, he sensed that it was going to be devastating.

"Damn!"

## Chapter Three

In Colorado, dressing down was "in." It was more commonly known as casual chic, but what that meant was jeans, boots, and cotton blouses. Lana had deliberated long and hard in Denver over what to bring with her. And she had finally thrown in a couple of silk dresses just for good measure, her reasoning being that if the lodge was as elegant as its prices indicated, she might need slightly dressier clothes. But as it turned out, "dressed for dinner" at Pine Lake Lodge meant nothing more than wearing a clean pair of jeans.

Lana had taken the tour of the stables with Dan and then relaxed in her claw-foot bathtub for a half hour before dressing for dinner in a soft brushed-denim skirt and a turquoise gauze blouse.

She was looking forward to this evening, hoping it would provide another angle of attack in the Senator Ryan story. But she first had to stop thinking about how nice the man's eyes were and how strong the grip of his hand was. She had to concentrate on what was important here—the senator's illegal connection in the bribery scandal.

When she entered the dining room, she was led by the headwaiter to a table in the center of the room and was seated with her back to John Ryan. But all it took was that short walk to the table once again to upset her equilibrium.

John was there, seated at a table by the window, and when he glanced up at her from across the room, their eyes met in a baffling mixture of suspicion and tempting fascination.

The feelings were new; different than the ones she had felt for Tom, and certainly more than a little disturbing. She tried to shake off the emotional grip that was beginning to tighten inside of her and instead concentrate objectively on the man. She noticed that John too had changed for dinner and was wearing brown corduroy slacks and a blue striped cotton shirt. But it was not his mode of dress that ingrained itself so on her mind in that short walk across the dining room. It was a vulnerability that she detected in him, a subtle crack in his carefully groomed public image that, she was beginning to decide, was only a shell.

John was looking out over the lake as if the view held some immutable law of the universe, but he wasn't seeing any of it. He had made the grave mistake of glancing toward the doorway at the very moment Lana Munsinger walked into the dining room.

He didn't want to be faced with the living presence of her. It was bad enough that he had thought of nothing and no one else all afternoon. It was the little things about her that kept whirling around in his mind like endless drops of warm water slapping at his skin and neck in a summer rain storm. It was her eyes, so green and penetrating, and that long mass of curly brown hair. And her voice. He especially liked that about her. It had surprised him when he'd first heard her speak. He had expected a typical reporter's grating, whining sound. But it had been soft and deeper than most women's voices, not masculine really, just full.

All of those little characteristics had been eating at him for several hours. They clouded his vision, blurred the bigger picture of who and what she was. He was suspicious, maybe overly so, but there was something about her that made him very nervous. He didn't want to lose track of that something, because then he could get caught in a relationship he had no time or inclination for.

Against his better judgment, he looked up to see where she was sitting. All he could see was her back, her curls resting lightly against the curve of her shoulders. Let it go, Ryan. Don't make more trouble for yourself than you can handle. He nervously fingered his glass of bourbon, thinking.

All right. He simply was not going to sit here and worry about what she was doing up here. No reporter was going to get the upper hand with him. This was his vacation and he was not going to spend the remaining days stewing over some imaginary threat. He was going to take care of this little problem here and now. He pushed his chair back forcefully and cut a determined path across the room.

Resting one hand on her table and the other on the back of her chair, John leaned close. "I don't recommend this table."

Lana had been perusing the menu, trying to decide what she wanted to eat. After seeing John Ryan, she wasn't sure if she could eat a bite. Her nerves were shot. But now, her startled gaze jerked from the menu in her hands to John's tight smile.

But, as surprised as she was to see him standing beside her, she was not going to show it. She retained a poker face, countering with reserve. "Oh, and why not?"

He leaned closer and she could smell the clean, fresh scent of his aftershave. And when he lowered his warm male voice, she felt an uncustomary tingling sensation along the back of her neck. "First of all, you've got the newlyweds at the table to your right. My room is next door to theirs and, believe me, you don't want to eat next to them. They'll drink too much champagne, giggle over absolutely nothing, and kiss throughout the entire meal."

John made a disgusted face and Lana arched her eyebrows, trying not to smile. "Hm, I see what you mean."

"If that were not enough, the man on your left is William Evanston." He rolled his eyes and Lana folded her arms, waiting for this next juicy tidbit of gossip. "You see that black bag on the table beside him?"

Lana shifted an undetected eye toward the man. "Yes?"

"Vitamins." John nodded with a knowing look.

Lana stared blankly. "So?"

"So!" John appeared astounded that she would question his point, but his mouth still remained close to her ear where only she could hear. "So, that's all he eats. That and a bowl full of mashed potatoes. Very unappetizing."

Lana leaned back in her chair and stared up at him, her lips hinting at a smile. "All right, Mr. Ryan, I'm convinced . . . now that I've thoroughly lost my appetite. So this isn't the table for me. Now what do you suggest?"

A shadow dropped over his face and spark of doubt flickered in the center of his eyes for an instant. He looked at her, hesitating, and then flashed a brittle campaign smile. "That you sit with me, of course."

She didn't answer for a few seconds, weighing

in her mind all the reasons why she should grab this opportunity to sit with him and get her story. This was her chance. This was the opening she had been looking for. But, strangely enough, she knew that none of these reasons were determining factors at all. "Am I to assume that hell has frozen over?"

He stared at her for a long moment, then smiled, still leaning close to her face. "Thawing," he said. "You see there must have been a temporary discontinuity in air mass properties where friction retarded the front near the ground. That tends to bring about a steeper frontal surface, causing gusty turbulent surface winds and—temporarily—colder temperatures."

"Ah, yes, of course." She shrugged. "Silly of me not to know. I should have guessed that right off."

A waiter stopped at Lana's table to ask if she'd like a frozen margarita. Lana lifted her eyes to John's face. "Yes, bring it to Mr. Ryan's table, please."

Eyeing him suspiciously, she stood. John put his hand on her left elbow and steered her toward his table, but Lana smiled shrewdly as her right hand moved, deftly and surreptitiously, to the interior of her purse, where she flicked the switch of her tape machine to Record.

John pulled out her chair for her and when she sat, his hand grazed her shoulder, igniting a liquid heat that ran like fire through her bloodstream.

"Isn't this better?" His smile held the intimacy of a warm summer night as he sat across from her, but the smile did not carry over to his eyes.

Lana didn't answer. She turned to look out the window at the valley wrapped in the soft light of evening. The lake lay in shadow and its color was now the same dark green as the pine trees that laced the meadow around it. A few windows were open and the rustle of wind in the trees and the pure, wholesome fragrance of pine caressed her already acute senses.

"It is beautiful, isn't it?" Her eyes filled with an iridescent reflection of the natural beauty around her.

"Heaven," he agreed.

Lana turned back to watch John as he gazed out the window and she once again detected a hint of vulnerability, as if this place, this view, offered him a solace he could find nowhere else.

Why did he ask her to sit with him? He obviously didn't like her much. Discontinuity in air mass properties. What a bunch of nonsense! "How do you know so much about weather?" Lana asked, folding her arms in front of her on the table.

"You happen to be sitting with ex-Lieutenant Ryan, ace weather forecaster for the U.S. Air Force."

Lana rolled her eyes. "How nice. Well at least

you'll have something to fall back on if you're defeated in the next election, won't you?''

"Interesting proposition that word *if.* I don't
put much stock in it actually."

"Aren't you afraid of too much confidence?
Just because you haven't lost an election yet...
there's always a first time for everything."

"How philosophical of you. I'll have to remember that for one of my campaign speeches."

Lana took a sip of the drink the waiter set before her and tried not to let Senator Ryan's re-
marks provoke her. She racked her brain for a
suitable comeback, but all of her caustic wit
seemed to be log-jammed in the back of her brain.

"I take it you wouldn't be too sick at heart if
my Democratic opponent trounced me." John
thanked the waiter for their drinks and began sipping lightly on his second bourbon.

"How perceptive of you. I'll have to remember
that for one of my articles," Lana smiled mischie-
vously.

John simply nodded. "Okay, so I've got a career in weather balloons and barometers waiting
for me. What do you have to fall back on if you
don't get your big story up here?"

Lana's eyes widened for a split second before
her expression was masked with indifference. But
her mind was racing a mile a minute. Did he suspect that she was here to get a story about him?
How could he possibly know? She opened her

mouth to recite her well-practiced line about re-searching her family's background, but for some reason, the words wouldn't come out as planned. When she did finally answer, the intensity of the one word was a painful surprise to both of them. "Nothing."

Lana was relieved from an explantion when another waiter arrived to take their dinner order. The menu changed every day, but each night there was a choice of three entrees and vege-tables, unless the kitchen was preparing your own special catch of trout, as it was doing tonight for John. And everything was served home style in big bowls of steaming potatoes, vegetables, platters of meat, and a large wooden bowl of salad.

"So you remember me badgering you at press conferences?" Lana asked as she took another sip of her drink.

John nodded. "Badger is too mild a term to use for what you and all your vigilant, persistent, sa-distic, and overly imaginative cohorts do to me in those sessions."

"Maybe you're just afraid to answer our ques-tions truthfully."

John's expression was clearly one of disgust. "The questions most of you ask and the subse-quent stories you write have nothing to do with truth."

"What is that supposed to mean?" Lana, whose

emotions were as transparent as glass, had never been good at hiding her anger.

"I mean the stories you write are your stories. They're your viewpoint, not mine, nor any other political figure's. There is little or no objectivity. It is all editorializing. For some reason, every journalist thinks he's a commentator."

"Just because you don't like what's being said...I mean we do have an obligation to let the public know what's going on. They have that right."

"That is the biggest crock of journalistic drivel I've ever heard. The right to know," he scoffed. "The right to know what? What I eat for breakfast? What I wear to bed? How far does it go?"

"Surely when you went into public office, you knew that you would be fair game." She took a hefty drink of her margarita, hoping it would calm the racing of her pulse.

"Sure, I knew that I would be expected to say what I thought about issues. They are important." He chuckled without humor. "I guess I was naïve, but I never expected to see them so twisted and manipulated. Hell, you know as well as I do that the issues are lost in all of the mumbo jumbo of hype and ratings and bylines. What are the issues anymore? Tell me, because I really don't know. I deal with them everyday, but I can't see them."

Lana watched John closely, surprised and intrigued to hear him speak so vehemently on the subject. *So he doesn't know the issues,* she thought wryly. *How interesting.* It was a new insight into the man. She would remember that for her story.

"You shouldn't take it so personally," she argued.

"But it is personal. Look what happened to Senator Aglestone a few months ago. Reporters and television crews were parked on his front lawn for weeks. His five year old daughter was followed to kindergarten by reporters who hoped to get a quote from her. A five year old, for Christ's sake! Now are you telling me that that's not personal?"

"Sam Aglestone was accused of a serious crime. The public had a right to know what was going on. And the reporters had a right to tell their stories. First amendment—freedom of speech, remember that one?"

"Yeah I've heard of it. But I've also heard of the right to privacy. And there should be such a thing as human decency. Why can't journalists try to be more human, try to think what their freedom of speech will do to a person's life and to his family's life? Don't you realize that the people you write about are human beings?"

Lana shrugged. "You're a public figure. You have an obligation to the people. And I, as a reporter, have an obligation to the people."

John stared at her, knowing she had understood nothing of what he was trying to say. She was just like every other damned reporter. Hatchet men, all of them. But he also was very aware of something else. Watching her beautiful, determined mouth and mesmerized by her brilliant green eyes, he had moved involuntarily into a phase of sexual hunger. His body had hardened solid with gnawing need and want for this woman he didn't even like, and his blood leapt like fire through his every artery and vein.

It was pure lust he was convinced, and yet he also sensed that it was something more. In all the years of his marriage, he and Anne had never debated over something like this. They'd had a multitude of different opinions, but had never cared enough to argue about any of them. She always just went her way and he went his. But here, with this woman he hardly knew, he was feeling argumentative and sexually aroused at the same time. What in the hell was she doing to him?

Lana was extremely uncomfortable. Senator Ryan was studying her, analyzing something about her, pulling her under him in some subtle sensual way that she couldn't seem to stop. She reached into her purse on the ruse of finding a tissue, but what she wanted was to touch her recorder, needing a reminder of what she was doing here, what she had to accomplish.

When the waiter set their food on the table and began dishing up helpings of zucchini and scalloped potatoes onto each plate, Lana shifted her attention away from John. She was learning too many things about him, things she really didn't want to know. And the more pertinent information she had come for was still only elusive conjecture. He claimed reporters invaded his privacy. Is that what she had come to do, invade a man's privacy? Right to privacy versus freedom of speech. What the hell was she getting into?

When the waiter left, an awkward silence hovered between the two of them. It was as if they had both come to the realization that a subtle change had taken place in both the real and the emotional air around them. Outside, a shift in the atmospheric pressure created a gust of wind which blew like a warm dry chinook down into the valley and through the open windows of the lodge.

To counteract the dynamic tension between them, Lana strove for nonchalance. "So, how much longer will you be here?"

John cut into the exquisitely prepared trout, as he tried to find an answer. He still wasn't sure what he was even doing here. He certainly hadn't come to any definite conclusions about his career yet. "I don't know. You?"

"I'm not sure yet. It all depends."

"On what?"

Lana shifted uncomfortably in her chair. She was supposed to be the one who conducted the interrogation. That was her job. But she suddenly felt as if she were strapped in a chair under hot lights and John Ryan was tightening the thumb screws.

"You've come to get a story about me, haven't you?"

Lana toyed with her food, avoiding his eyes. Finally she looked up, but there was anything but confidence in her eyes. "Yes."

The corners of his mouth turned down and he nodded his head slowly. "I see. Is it okay to ask what you're after? What provocative scoop you are on to?"

"Abscam." She watched him closely and didn't miss the flinch. There was a small snap of his jaw muscle and a flash of surprise in his eyes. But, more than surprise, they held a look of defeat.

He set his fork down slowly, exhaling a long, even breath. Now he knew why he had been cautious, why he had been wary of her from the beginning. And now he knew why he should have remained that way. Male-female relationships were an emotional drain. He had learned that the hard way. And he had vowed not to fall into that trap again. But in one afternoon, with the air crisp, the sun brilliant, and the scent of nature wafting through his body, he had let this woman crawl under his skin. He had dropped his guard for a few brief moments and had given her the opportunity to strike with her poisonous venom.

John narrowed his eyes on her, wanting to find something ugly and devious and hateful about her. He tried to demote his feelings for her to the prurient stage, but he couldn't. There was something about her that was as soft and fresh and enticing as the warm seductive evening around them. And, for some inexplicable reason, he wanted her more than he had ever wanted a woman in his life.

"I did nothing illegal." John paused and she waited, breathless and still, for him to continue. He took note of the look in her eyes, that glazed need to hear it all. She would write it and her readers would devour it, getting a vicarious thrill out of seeing someone else's dirty laundry. "I don't have to explain a damn thing to you."

He looked as if he were going to say something more, so Lana continued to wait. But a few seconds later he slapped his napkin onto the table, pushed back his chair, and left the dining room.

Lana didn't look up. She stared at her plate of barely touched food. Then she looked at his plate, at his expertly prepared trout that he had caught this afternoon. A wave of regret and nausea attacked her midsection and for the first time ever, she was almost sorry she had stumbled on to a promising lead for a story.

She stuck her fork into the tender salmon and mechanically lifted it to her mouth, and never once during the whole meal did she taste a bite of it.

Lana lay at an angle across her bed, hugging the calico pillow to her chest. She was trying, and had been trying for the last hour and a half, to rid her mind of the nagging doubts that assailed her. She rolled over onto her stomach and buried her face in the pillow.

What was the matter with her? Why did she feel this disgust with herself? This wasn't the first exposé she had ever worked on. She was a journalist. It was her job to weed out the facts, however incriminating or ruinous they might be to the person or persons involved. It was her job, damn it!

She pushed from the bed and paced the room, vacillating between embarrassment and anger. A journalist was supposed to remain objective, not become personally involved in a story. But then, it wasn't the story she was drawn to; it was the man.

She flung the pillow furiously toward the bed. John Ryan, of all people! That conservative, buttoned-down champion of the unprogressive and immoral status quo. She detested what his family's mining operations had done to the ecological balance of this state and other western states. The gouging, the stripping, the contamination of lakes and streams, much of it by the hand of Ryan Resources.

And yet...and yet...a sensual heat slithered up the insides of her thighs at the thought of what "yet" implied.

But why was she afflicted with a profession that would put her in this position! She couldn't help but wonder if her father or his father or grandfather had ever been in this position, choosing between a story and a person who meant something special to them. She had believed for so many years that her career was the only thing that mattered. For a while after Tom died, it was the only thing that had given her a reason to be.

Besides, she had been raised with a reverence for and an excitement for curiosity, with the creed of the Munsinger family being Who, What, Where, When, and Why. There simply was no other choice.

And yet....

John stood on the deck with one foot propped up on the railing. The wind still moving down from the tops of the mountains was unseasonably warm. Heavy clouds hung over the peaks, resulting in a dry downslope of air into the valley. The moon winding in and out of the clouds was reflected in the water of the lake below and the entire valley lay in dark, almost somber tranquility. But John's thoughts were anything but tranquil.

He was wondering at exactly what point his life got away from him. To what year could he go back and start anew? Twenty-five? Twenty-six? After his tour of duty in the service, he had gone back to complete his last two years of law school. He had been so full of anticipation then, full of plans for the future. The law office he was going to open in a small town west of Denver. The log house he was going to build in the mountains. The woman he would find, fall in love with, and marry. The children he would teach to fish, and hike, and build snow caves.

Funny, he thought. None of those dreams came to pass. Not even one of them. But then, he hadn't been forced into a life with Anne or into a chaotic political life that left no room for anything or anyone else. No one had twisted his arm. It had been offered, that's all. It would be easy, he was told. Financial backers were waiting, publicity promoters were enthusiastic, campaign strategists were optimistic. He could have said no, but he didn't. He said yes to it all. To the candidate makers. To Anne Bouchard, the socially and politically expedient catch of the season. To a life shuttling back and forth from Washington to Denver. To parties with all the right people. To mud-slinging, and logrolling, and charismatic ambiguity and wordplay.

But now he wondered why. Maybe he was just going through that time of life, that middle-age crazy stage. Or perhaps it was more than that. Whatever it was, it had him hiding out in the mountains, away from the world he was supposed to help govern, and scared to death of his feelings about a beautiful, overzealous reporter who was up here with the sole purpose of ruining him. He closed his eyes briefly and felt again the sting of desire penetrating his skin.

Why didn't he just go upstairs and knock on Justine Moreau's door? He had certainly been given enough encouragement from her. And that way he could forget about Lana Munsinger for a little while. He needed time to think about what and how much he should tell her. If he told her the truth, would she believe it or would she submit the story that was already in her mind? Oh, who could tell what devious things rumbled around in those journalistic minds!

Lana opened the french doors that led from the lobby to the deck. It was quiet out at this late hour. Most of the guests were either playing cards, reading in the lobby, or they had turned in for the night.

As she stepped onto the deck, she breathed in the warm, dry air. This really was a lovely spot, isolated, insulated, and peaceful. It would be nice if she could relax and really enjoy it. But the prospects for that looked grim indeed. Things were not happening the way she expected at all. She had planned to come up to the lodge, find Ryan, confront him immediately with her accusa-

tions, and get a juicy, incriminating quote in response. Where did she go wrong?

If he were unattractive, she certainly wouldn't
have any problem justifying her means to the
story. Or if he were stupid, or sarcastic, or unkind.
But he was none of those things. Even so, she had
been around handsome, brilliant men before.
What was so different about this one? *Oh, Lana,
you idiot! You're not in the market for a man. You had
one once. But since then, you've established a good
life for yourself. Don't screw it up now. Get your story
and get back to the life you're familiar with.*

Lana continued to walk around the deck, expe-
riencing the view from every side of the lodge.
When the moon slipped behind the clouds, it was
so dark she could barely see a foot in front of her.
But when the clouds rolled back, the mountains
loomed dark and big and very close.

She turned the last corner and saw a lone figure
on the deck, his hands supporting his weight
against the railing. She new immediately who it
was. Already his lean build and handsome profile
had taken up residence in her mind, and it would
take more than physical distance for it to move
away. He was still wearing the same clothes he'd
worn to dinner, but his hair was now tousled by
the loving caress of the breeze.

He looked up just as she came around the
corner and she knew there was no avoiding him
now. Some impertinent circuit in the back of her

mind insisted that this was what she had come downstairs for in the first place.

She walked toward him and stopped only a foot or so away. *Okay, Lana, don't say anything stupid like "hi." Say something brilliant, or witty, or probing. Think about what one of those other imminent Munsingers would say in this situation.*

"Hi." Oh, damn! she groaned inwardly and wished she could crawl into the woodwork where she belonged.

"Hello." John's hand clutched the railing, more for emotional support than physical. He couldn't expect to hide from her forever. This lady was going to expect some explanations. "Looks like it's going to rain tonight or tomorrow."

"Yes, you're probably right."

"It should cool things off a bit."

"Yes."

John expelled a full breath. Well, enough avoidance. They might as well get this over with. "Guess you have some questions to ask."

"A few." She hesitated, not even sure she wanted to know the truth. Ignorance is bliss, they always say. And since meeting this man, she was beginning to believe "they" were right. "Were you involved in Abscam?"

"Yes. And no."

"Is that some sort of political paradox?" What did he think he was trying to pull with her? She certainly hoped he wasn't going to take her for a fool. A little campaign smile here and some clever equivocation there was not going to disrupt this reporter's equilibrium. Not much anyway.

"No, it's the truth." He paused, glancing down at her hands. "Where's your tape recorder?"

Lana flinched and straightened her shoulders. How had he known? And why hadn't he said anything at dinner about it? "I don't need it."

"Good. What I'm trying to say is that I did nothing illegal." He took a deep breath and blew it out between puffed cheeks wondering once again where all of this was going to lead. "I have earned a certain amount of clout in the Senate over the last few years...." He stopped and smiled for the first time since she'd walked up to him. "I'm sure there are those who feel that clout is unwarranted. Am I right?"

"I think I'll plead the Fifth Amendment on that one," Lana answered, smiling back at him. "Let's just say I'm aware of the fact."

"Well, anyway, as it turned out the FBI seemed to think they could use my influential charisma or whatever it is I supposedly have in their little scam."

"You mean you were in on it from the beginning?"

"That's right. They contacted me about two months before they set everything into motion. They wanted me to plant a seed with certain senators—you know, drop a few hints about deals being made with the Arabs. Hell, all I really had to do was attend a few parties, sprinkle a few names in the right places. It didn't seem like much to ask at the time. I never actually said I had made a deal with anyone, but of course in Washington innuendo is the name of the game."

Lana shook her head, then gazed up at the moon as it did its disappearing act behind a curtain of clouds.

"You don't believe me." John cocked his head, then lifted a boot to the lower rung of the railing.

Lana turned back to him, staring into the fathomless depths of his eyes, trying to divine what was the truth and what was not. "I didn't say that. However, you do have to admit that's it's pretty incredible. Sounds a little too much like the childhood game of Follow the Leader."

John frowned and turned his gaze toward the direction of the lake. "The adult term is entrapment."

Lana didn't fail to catch the tight snap of his jaw, the physical manifestation of his own doubts over the course of action he took.

"I didn't particularly want to do it—trick my congressional colleagues. Besides, I was afraid this thing could backfire in my face and I'd end up at the very least looking like a horse's ass and at the very worst in jail." He looked at Lana and gave her a poor attempt at a smile. "Looks like I may end up that horse's rear-end after all."

"Why did you go along with the plan?" Lana asked, trying quickly to override the shadows of guilt that were starting to emerge from the dark and stalk around her.

He stared down at the tip of his boot protruding through the rail, and he shook his head. "I'm not really sure. Maybe it was because for years I sat on the Senate Ethics Committee and—hell, as self-righteous as it sounds, I just couldn't let it go. If there were some bad apples in Congress, I wanted them out." He smiled again at her, and this time it was genuine. "It does sound pretty incredible, doesn't it?"

Lana relaxed her shoulders and sat down on the rail facing him. "It certainly does." She sat silent for a moment, then asked, "Was it worth it?"

"That's a hard thing to judge. I knew I was taking a risk, but I thought I was doing the right thing. Who's to say? A lot of people are opposed to entrapment as a means of establishing guilt. And they're right... to a point. But at the same time if we can't keep our own lawmakers honest, we're headed for even worse trouble."

"Are you going to run for President on a law and order ticket?"

"President!" John laughed, and the sound wound through her nerves like molten silver. "Don't you think you're jumping the gun a little?"

"Well, your name is brought up frequently as a

potential contender for the next presidential election.''

"Talk, that's all it is.''

"Are you saying you won't try for the bid?''

John leaned close to her and Lana could smell the woodsy scent of his aftershave. His shirt was open at the collar and she had the almost uncontrollable desire to lay her hand against his neck, to feel the warmth of his flesh. "That, Lana, is another topic altogether. If and when I decide, I promise you that you'll be the first to know.''

Lana felt a heated flush crawl along her skin, and it had nothing to do with his comment and everything to do with his nearness. She strove desperately for nonchalance. "Would it do that much damage to your career if the story about Abscam came out?''

"Probably.''

"How do I know you're telling me the truth?''

He stared down at her. She was so close. All he would have to do is lean down just a bit more and he could taste the mouth he had fantasized about all day. She smelled so good, not that overpowering synthetic smell of Justine Moreau, but rather like the pine trees and the moisture-laden clouds, natural and very seductive.

"You don't know,'' he answered in a voice so low she was forced to lean closer. "But if you're the reporter I think you are, you'll check out the facts before you write the story.''

"I will check it out, you know," she whispered, trying to swallow the almost strangling lump of emotions that seemed to block her throat.

"I know that."

"I have to follow this lead." She watched his face move closer and she closed her eyes in anticipation.

"Yes, and I have to follow this lead." He closed the gap between them, pressing his lips against hers.

An avalanche of sensations tumbled down through her body, a whirling mass of fear and excitement and desire. She invited the increasing pressure and she offered no resistance when he reached around her with his arm and pulled her up against his body.

They stood together on the deck as the clouds continued to roll in and neither was aware of anything but the warmth of arms and hands that encircled and stroked. Her mouth opened under the guidance of his and she was aware of a billowing storm that formed in the center of her body. His tongue stroked deep and intimate and she pressed her hips closer to his in response.

When he moved his mouth to her ear, he whispered her name and a hot chill ran the length of her spine. Expecting another sensual onslaught from his lips, she was surprised when John stepped back, turned away, and rested both hands against the railing. Lana stood beside him, both of them silent for a long, haunting moment, each looking out into the fragmented specters of imperfect pasts that lurked in the darkness.

Lana felt as if a serrated knife had passed through her abdomen and left her shredded with a mixture of unfulfilled desire and confusion. She had never felt this all consuming need for a man before. She and Tom had had a good sexual relationship, but it was nothing compared to the sensations that boiled a path through her bloodstream now.

She glanced sideways at John's serious, well-chiseled profile and she wondered if he too had some ghosts with which to deal. He had been married for many years and Lana had read enough about his wife to know what life with her must have been like. Still, maybe he was one of those who clung to what was or what might have been. One of those who could never forget or get over the past. Maybe he even still loved her. Lana shuddered and turned back to the dark shadows that danced among the pine trees.

John straightened, pushing himself away from the edge of the deck, away from Lana. He looked down at her and didn't smile. "It's very important that this story doesn't reach the press, Lana. I'm not asking for myself. But there are other lives involved. So . . . I hope to hell you'll turn out to be one of an all but extinct breed—a responsible journalist."

He turned and walked away, through the double doors of the lobby, and Lana followed his retreating figure with eyes that stung with bewilderment and blurred even more the image of who and what Senator John Ryan was.

# Chapter Four

Morning came early up this high: delicate pale light that traversed the mountain tops, clear sounds of dawn emitted by water cascading over rocks as the snow melted up even higher than the lodge, and by pine and aspen trees waking to a rustling breeze. The meadows of grass and wildflowers were still damp from the night's rain, but the sky was crystal blue, and not a cloud remained in sight.

Lana was already up, calling a friend who worked as a correspondent on Capitol Hill in Washington, frantically trying to salvage what little was left of her story. She had lain awake for hours last night with the opposing scenes tossing and turning in her mind—John's explanation of his role in Abscam, then his mouth and hands so hot and insistent against her, and finally his abrupt withdrawal into impenetrable reserve.

Now she had to make sense of it all in the only way she knew how. Her editor would be expecting her call today and she would have to have some information for him. So, she now sat on the edge of the bed waiting impatiently for her contact in Washington to answer his phone.

Her contact? Is that all Matthew Grimes was to her now, an impersonal business associate? He had been so much more at one time.

Lana's mind traveled back across the years, picking and choosing among the pieces of memory that lay like a baffling jigsaw puzzle with too many ragged and bent edges. Yes, Matthew had been more. Much more. He had been Tom's best friend. A flicker of sadness darted along the rim of her conscience as the phone rang three times before being answered.

"Matthew? This is Lana ... Lana Munsinger."

A long pause tore even deeper into her body. "Lana ... hello. I haven't heard from you in a while. Been on a big story?"

She brushed the pain away. "Oh, yeah, Matthew, you bet." She frowned as she thought of her last big story. "Ling Lang, the Denver Zoo's oldest orangutan gave birth a month ago, and yours truly got to cover it."

Matthew chuckled, but there was little humor in the sound. "I suppose that's the reward of four years of college."

There was a hesitation between the two of them that hadn't been there when Tom was alive. Then they had all three been best buddies. The Three

Musketeers, they used to call themselves. But no more.

"Those four years seem awfully short now," Lana said, a wistful tone echoing through her words. "Do you ever wish we could go back and start over, Matt?"

"I try not to think too much about it." His voice had grown cold and distant, and Lana swallowed the defeat she felt. Did Matthew blame her in some way for Tom's death?

It had been such a crazy kaleidoscopic time for the world and for Lana. She and Tom met their first year in college and, in a blind fit of passion and young love, had married. Tom was not doing well in school and flunked out during the first semester of their sophomore year. Lana had continued with her courses and worked at the journalism school while Tom worked in a convenience store to help pay the rent. When the draft notice came in the mail, Tom and his best friend Matthew were stunned. But Lana had been raised in a conservative family where patriotism was one step behind sainthood, so for her it was a chance for her husband to do his duty to his country. Matthew, on the other hand, thought the whole idea of war immoral and stupid. Go to Canada, he insisted. You're crazy to let them draft you and ship you over to Nam. But Tom, easygoing and optimistic about what life would offer him, decided to take his chances with the draft.

When he reported for his physical, a loud, burly sergeant marched down the line counting "one, two, three, marine. One, two three, marine." Being number four in the sequence, Tom was chosen to be one of "The few, the proud."

It really wasn't so bad, they both decided. She had glowed with pride as she sat in the audience and watched him graduate from the boot camp at LeJeune. And even when he got his assignment for Vietnam, they were both optimistic. "I'm going to be a computer programmer, Lannie. How dangerous can that be!"

He was stationed at Red Beach, south of Da Nang, where at night he had to take his turn guarding the perimeter of the compound. But he glossed over all of that in his letters, painting instead a glowing picture of rain-soaked forests where the early morning mists had an ethereal, enchanting quality, of roach killing contests between the marines in his hut and the others in the compound, and always, always of simple, safe computer programming.

She had flown to Hawaii to meet him for his R & R and those two weeks were the most blissful of her life. The two of them swam and ate and laughed and made love and completely forgot that two thousand miles away, young lives were being snuffed out in a game of war that seemed to have no end and very few rules.

The last time she saw Tom was when he boarded the plane back to Da Nang, with his reassurance of a safe computer programming assignment echoing in her ears. Two weeks later, she received a telegram. It had happened while he was asleep. The Viet Cong had dropped a mortar shell into the camp and all of the occupants of Tom's hut were killed instantly. A month later, the President ordered the withdrawal of all American troops from Vietnam.

She had encouraged her husband to become a soldier. And he had died because of it. Maybe Matthew was right. Maybe it was her fault. Oh, but she had been over it all so many times in the past. Rehashed it, changed the mold, bent the actualities into possibilities until she had finally learned to accept the reality. It had stopped mattering a long time ago whose fault it was. It was over and there was no sense trying to rewrite the script.

"What can I do for you, Lana?" Matt's tone, professionally cool and distant, brought Lana back to the present.

"I wanted to check out a lead I had the other day concerning John Ryan." *Yes, Lana, business to the forefront as usual. It's better that way.*

"Senator Ryan?"

"Yes. It's about Abscam."

"You're going back aways. That's old news."

"Maybe not. I heard that Ryan was implicated, but it was never brought to the public eye." Lana had used the strong term *implicated* on purpose, hoping to trigger an honest reaction from Matthew. And it worked.

"Implicated! No way. Listen, the way I understood it—and my source of information is always reliable—was that Ryan was in on the deal from the beginning. He was used as bait for some of the other congressmen, that's all. It wasn't publicized because first of all, it would turn a lot of people off to Ryan. They'd think of him in terms of entrapment, you see. Secondly, part of his terms were that his name wouldn't be released. The FBI had no choice if they wanted his cooperation."

"Damn." Lana began biting on the end of one of her nails. There went her exposé. All shot to hell!

"Don't tell me you were planning a story around that."

Lana's silence said it all.

"Hell, Lana, why didn't you call me when you first heard about it? I could have set you straight."

Lana thought carefully before she spoke. "I... sometimes I hesitate calling you Matt."

"I see."

*Do you, Matthew? Do you see it at all?* "It triggers some... well, you know, some unpleasant memories."

"Yes, I do know. It does for me too." His voice was stiff and formal and the lack of affectionate empathy between them plunged like ice into her heart. But did she have the right to expect more? They were not the same people they once were. Tom had been the cohesive element that had held the three of them together. Without him, the bond was gone. She could relate to Matthew on a business level, but beyond that, there was nothing. She might as well accept that the gap between them was too wide ever to fill again. "Well, thank you, Matt."

"Sure, anytime," he answered too quickly, too casually, and when Lana hung up the phone, she was left with a hollow ache in the pit of her stomach.

There were times when the friendly past refracted across her mind's eye like the deflection of light through crystal, spreading the spectrum of color from younger days when the three of them had been carefree and unaware of death. But this was not one of those times. It all happened almost eleven years ago and so many things had changed since then. The world had grown and moved into its cyclical phase of military R & R. Right now, the country felt no need to flex its muscles before the rest of the world. It was at peace.

Lana too had changed and was no longer at war with her emotions. She had adjusted to life

without Tom, had grown more liberal in her out-
look every year, and had built a fulfilling, re-
warding life of her own, with problems of its
own. She closed her eyes and sighed. Foremost
among those problems was this story about John
Ryan.

Deep inside, she was subconsciously relieved
that he had done nothing illegal, and yet she knew
that Walter was going to be very upset because
she hadn't checked out her facts better before
coming up here. Upset was too mild a term, she
conceded. He was going to boil her in oil! She
could already hear his raging anger bellowing in
her mind. *And why didn't you check out these
facts before you left for this godforsaken mountain retreat, Munsinger? Huh?*

Oh, dear. She knew she should call him and get
it over with, but... well, maybe she'd organize
her shoes in the closet first.


"So how are the funds holding out?" Dan leaned
back in his chair, so the waiter could pick up his
breakfast plate.

John picked up his cup and sipped at the steaming coffee. "Okay, I guess. My manager insists
that I shouldn't even concern myself with something as mundane as campaign funds. 'Just make
yourself lovable, Ryan,' he keeps telling me."
John grinned. "So what do you think, Dan, am I a
lovable guy or not?"

"Indeed you are," Dan laughed, slapping his

napkin to the table and pushing back his chair. "But you're also as transparent as glass."

John paused before buttering another biscuit. "What do you mean?"

"I mean your heart isn't in this election, is it?"

John buttered his biscuit slowly, setting the knife down carefully on his plate, before looking back at Dan. "No, not really."

Dan nodded and stood to leave, scooted his chair toward the table, and rested his hand on its back. "So if it's not in the election, where is it?" He didn't wait for an answer, but turned and walked toward the lobby, stopping at another table to chat with some of his guests.

The biscuit was suspended in the air between John's plate and his mouth. His heart? Where was his heart? He felt a spark of electricity in his gut as he thought of Lana Munsinger and the way her hands clung to the back of his neck and hair last night, the feel of her pelvis pressed tightly against his, the surrender of her mouth to his tongue. And then he thought of his father and the tenuous thread of life that held his seventy-year-old heart together. What would the story about Abscam do to him? Dan was right, his heart wasn't in the election. That was the least of his worries. But where was it? Good question, Dan.

"It's about time you called me, Munsinger." *Dear, sweet Walter. Always the same.* "Well, what have you got?"

Lana unconsciously wiped a few beads of sweat from her upper lip. "I've run into a little bit of a snag, Walt. Ryan wasn't involved."

"What do you mean 'wasn't involved'?"

She knew she should tell him about John's actual involvement in Abscam, even though it wasn't illegal. But, Walter might possibly decide to print it anyway. Since it wasn't really the news-breaking item she had originally thought it would be, there wasn't much point in telling Walter at all. After all, there was no reason to rake the senator over the coals if it wasn't necessary. Oh, Lana, whom do you think you're fooling!

"I mean my source was wrong."

"If this is your idea of an early morning prank, Munsinger, I fail to see the humor. Now where's the story?"

Lana grabbed the morning newspaper that had been delivered to her door and began fanning herself in earnest. "There is no story, Walter."

"This is the third time you've done this to me, Munsinger." Walter's voice dropped to a deadly decibel and Lana knew she was in trouble. As long as he was bellowing, everything was relatively okay, but when his voice was quiet and low, everyone in the newsroom grew very nervous. "The third story that you've gone off half-cocked and then ended up with nothing." he continued. "I've been fair. Because of your family's distin-guished background, and your father's influence with certain members of this establishment, I've given you more than your fair share of chances. But I will give you no more.''

"Walt, it wasn't my fault!"

He forged ahead, ignoring her flimsy excuse entirely. "I am paying out the nose for you to hang out in that lodge in the boonies. I am paying for you to bring me something newsworthy on Senator Ryan. Now you will either have something for me in forty-eight hours or I will have your desk cleaned out and your things will be stacked in the lobby of the building for you to pick up when you get back to town. Do I make myself clear?"

Lana's hand had lost all circulation where it gripped the phone so tightly, and the newspaper had fallen uselessly to the floor. Her job! She was actually going to lose her job over this? This was everything she had ever worked for. Lana Munsinger fired! A Munsinger who couldn't cut it as a journalist? No! She would not let that happen. John Ryan was just a temporary disgression, one she was sure she could avoid if she tried a little harder, but this job was her whole life. "I understand, Walter. I'll get you a story."

"Forty-eight hours, Munsinger."

"Yes. Forty-eight hours."

Lana sat on the edge of the bed for several agonizing minutes before she could force herself to stand and walk into the bathroom. She looked at herself in the mirror and felt faint. When had life become so confusing? For so many years now, it had seemed so simple. She had adjusted to Tom's death, her father got her this wonderful job, she was working her way up to a position of prominence. What happened? John Ryan, that's what happened, she bleakly reminded herself.

She clipped her hair back then leaned over the sink and began washing her face, and the frigid temperature of the water sent a chill scurrying along the surface of her skin. How could it have happened? How could she have let that man upset her equilibrium so?

Well, he had done enough damage already, she decided as she dried her face with a towel. She was simply going to go downstairs, confront him with—well, she'd decide what on the way downstairs—then she would force some hidden ghost from his closet. She was going to get this story!

Lana checked her pale peach blouse and blue gauze skirt in the full-length mirror one more time before she picked up her room key and headed downstairs. Her stride was determined and her face was set in an unconquerable pose, but when she stood in the doorway of the restaurant and watched John Ryan reading the newspaper at his table across the room, her shoulders drooped tiredly and her victorious expression fell into folds of defeat. *Sure, Lana, you're just going to walk across the room and confront him like Attila the Hun, right? Wrong.* Just the sight of him from twenty feet away left her muscles weak and flaccid and her motivation dried up.

*Pick up your feet and walk over there, Lana. Pick up your feet.* She swiveled around sharply and walked as quickly as possible to the other side of the lobby.

She stood against the far wall of the lobby, staring up at the huge Kodiak bear fur that hung on the wall above her. She couldn't do it. She just couldn't single out John Ryan for an abusive attack that had no basis. If she had to write about him, maybe she could find something nice to say, a heartwarming human interest piece maybe. *Oh, that's a good one, Lana. I'd like to see Walter print something like that.* The unofficial motto around the office was "Let's go for the grit." Get a revealing quote from some distraught widow, smear a candidate's face in his own defeat, drag the goriest details of a train wreck across the front pages. That's what the public wanted to read. Sensationalism and innuendo. Headlines that screamed out at them, shaking the foundations of their snug little worlds. But surely a pleasant, upbeat story was in order now and then.

Lana spun back around, searching the lobby for a phone. She'd call Chuck. That's what she'd do. He was the one who gave her the information about John in the first place, and if anyone had any information about senators from Colorado, it would be Chuck. And after all, what were friends for? She had known him since they were in kindergarten. He wouldn't let her down.

Lana located the phone and took a deep breath before picking it up to dial.

John Ryan had looked up from his paper in time to see Lana Munsinger fleeing from the restaurant. He frowned, debating with himself. Maybe he should see where she went, try to talk to her again. No, that didn't work out too well last night. Being around her put his libido into overdrive and turned him into an inarticulate idiot. Besides, would it really do any good to talk to her? This was one decision she was going to have to make herself.

He folded his paper and stood to leave, but Dan stopped him as he was walking toward the door. "I'm going to be taking several people up to see some of the mining sites today, John. You want to go? To be quite honest with you," Dan whispered, "the Rappaports from St. Louis are going and I could use some sane company."

John laughed. He had planned to fish again today, but hell, why not? "Sure, I'll go. What time?"

"Thanks, buddy." Dan slapped the younger man's shoulder in relief. "We'll leave in an hour."

"Damn it, Lana, I thought I told you not to talk about this stuff over the phone. I could get in a hell of a lot of trouble over this."

"Look, Chuck, I'll owe you forever, okay? I'll pay you back somehow, I promise."

"How?"

"Give me a break, Chuck. I don't know . . . somehow."

"Well, what if I don't have anything to tell you anyway?"

"Then I'll kill you. How's that?" Lana snapped, too tired to play games at this stage.

"The only thing I know about Ryan is what I hear his ex-wife say. She's blabbing tacky things all over the city."

"What do you mean? In Denver? Anne Ryan is in Denver?"

Chuck sighed, obviously reluctant to tell her anything. "Yes. Doing publicity on her new book."

"Where's she staying?"

"Say please."

"Oh, for heaven's sake, Chuck. Oh, all right, please," she drawled with a nasty twang.

"At the Hyatt."

Lana was just replacing the phone in its cradle when the shadow of Dan Granger loomed large and imposing beside her. His eyes spoke clearly of the fact that he'd overheard her conversation, but his voice was that of the perfect host.

"Good morning, Lana. Sleep all right?"

"Yes," she lied. She hadn't slept worth a darn. "Thank you."

"I was just wondering if you'd like to see some of those mining sites today."

"Mining sites?" She looked baffled for a split second, before managing to recover sufficiently. "Oh, mining sites. Of course, that sounds... great." She had completely forgotten that she was supposed to be researching her great-grandfather's history up here in the mountains. But Dan Granger certainly hadn't forgotten and he was going to make sure she got what she supposedly came for and nothing else. Lana nervously checked her watch. If she spent the day doing this, that would only leave her about thirty-six hours to get her story for Walter. "What time are we going?" She tried to muster some enthusiasm, but her smile was tight and strained.

"At ten o'clock. Out front."

"Okay. I'll be there." She watched Dan walk away then, with something less than total certainty, Lana placed a call to the Hyatt Regency Hotel in Denver.

## Chapter Five

After the night's rain, the air was much cooler than the day before, and it had that fresh washed smell that heightened the natural scent of pine and wild rose. The clouds had disssipated and the sun shone brightly on the few patches of snow that still covered the tips of the mountains.

Lana had gone back to her room to change into soft, stone-washed jeans and a rust plaid shirt and was the last one to arrive at the front of the lodge for the day-long excursion. She stopped on the top step of the porch, staring at the four-wheel drive that was being loaded for the day trip. Dan was helping a middle-aged couple to climb into the seat directly behind the driver's while John Ryan packed some tools and a couple of fishing rods into the back of the wagon.

John looked up as she walked toward the truck and his expression was as stunned as hers. Both stood still for several moments, working out plausible excuses in their minds for not going on this tour. Lana spoke first.

"I didn't know who was going with Dan today."

"Neither did I." John loaded a heavy metal box of tools into the truck and closed the tail gate firmly.

Neither of them said that if they had known each other was going, they would have declined, but the words were there in the silence that followed. For Lana, this whole day was going to be a big waste of time. If only she had told Dan she was coming to the lodge to meditate. But the story about her great-grandfather and his adventures in these mountains had been the first thing to come to mind. And now she was going to be faced with John Ryan all day. Would she be able to maintain a professional distance between them, or would the feelings that kept rising unwillingly to the surface of her skin betray what little control she had left around this man?

At least tomorrow she would be doing something constructive on her article. She had called Anne Ryan in Denver this morning and set up an interview for one o'clock tomorrow afternoon. Anne Ryan's name and opinions had been in the news for years, but she was now entering a whole new arena. The publishing industry. She had written a novel, and though the publisher was inundating the public with lots of advance publicity, the senator's ex-wife was going to cash in on all the attention she could get. So, when a reporter from the *Rocky Mountain News* contacted her, she was more than willing to set up an appointment with Lana.

She glanced sideways at John, a shaft of guilt wedging between her ribs. Should she tell him that she was no longer planning an article about Abscam, but that she was looking for another angle through his ex-wife?

Before she could broach the subject, Dan walked back to join them. He was holding a picnic basket in his hand and a thermos under the crook of his arm. "You two ready to go?" he asked, setting the basket and thermos down on the ground so that he could reopen the tailgate. Being around him, it was easy to forget his physical limitations. Dan never expected anyone to do anything for him and it seemed as if there were nothing he couldn't do himself. Lana liked him a lot, but she sensed a certain wariness in his eyes whenever he was around her. "Let's go." He closed up the back of the vehicle and walked around to the driver's seat.

The front passenger seat was taken by a man from Tucson, Arizona, whose lap was overflowing with camera equipment. Even the floor in front of him held his tripod, cases of film, and lenses.

There was only one seat left, so Lana reluctantly slid into the rear bench seat and John followed her. In a not-so-subtle attempt to avoid physical contact, Lana laid her jacket on the seat between them.

The Rappaports from St. Louis sat directly in front of them and provided everyone with some levity on the trip. They were both overweight, loud, and at constant odds with each other. "Put your coat over here with mine, Sidney. No, it takes up too much space there. Here, with mine. That's better. Now roll up your sleeves, dear, you'll get too hot."

"I am not too hot, Agnes."

"No, but you will be. In an hour you'll be complaining about how hot you are."

"I will not, Agnes."

"You will, Sidney. I know you. You will."

With a heaving sigh of surrender, Sidney rolled up his sleeves to appease his wife.

"Now look out the window, Sidney. You don't want to miss anything."

Sidney turned, silently praying for a few moments respite from his wife's constant nagging.

Lana shook her head and smiled, and when she glanced at John she noticed that he was grinning too. He held out his hand to her. "You think we should call a truce for today? I mean we are going to be together for several hours and...I'm not very comfortable with this constrained silence. Are you?"

"No." Her mouth lifted in a sheepish smile as she placed her hand in his. "Truce." But at that point, the casual companionship ended. Tiny beads of restless need slipped through her pores and followed the migratory network of veins through her body, and her pulse began to thunder in her ears. Her gaze moved restlessly to the view beyond the windows as she tried to cover the feelings that were so raw and exposed before him.

John pulled his hand back, emotionally bruised by the mere contact of their hands. This was ridiculous. He was a grown man. He'd known many women in his life. What was so special about this one? She didn't even like him, for God's sake! And to top it all off, she was out for blood!

A tortuous vision of the past fifteen years intersected his present thoughts. His marriage, if it could be called that, had been loveless from the beginning. And, although Anne had inconvenienced him publicly and privately more times than he cared to remember, it had essentially been a marriage of convenience. He had certainly never had to work to keep her. She had just always been there. Pushy, ambitious, and bitingly cold.

Lana Munsinger was ambitious too. That much was obvious. But still, what a difference between the two women! They were absolutely nothing alike. Lana was determined, yes. Maybe even a little pushy. But not cold. Never that. John forced himself not to look at the woman next to him. He even tried to relax in the seat and enjoy the scenery, but his every cell was buzzing with her nearness.

Dan wound through the mountains, leading the four-wheel drive wagon through narrow passes and across steep ledges that clung precariously to the sides of cliffs. The morning turned out to be a glorious montage of fresh air, sparkling clean streams, shimmering aspen leaves, and fragrant pine trees. An unspoiled paradise that seemed totally oblivious of the clamor of the twentieth century.

Mr. Fisch from Tucson continuously hung out the window with his camera. The man spent several minutes preparing for each shot, adjusting and realigning his focus, and at the precise moment the shutter clicked, Dan would inevitably hit a boulder or drop into a deep chuck hole. He insisted that he would be happy to stop the truck if only Mr. Fisch would let him know when he wanted to take a picture. But Mr. Fisch cheerfully dismissed the offer and continued clicking away at the bouncy blur of scenery.

While the cheery photographer snapped pictures, the Rappaports bickered and fussed with their belongings, John and Lana tried to ignore the nearness of each other's bodies, and Dan played the role of tour guide.

"We won't have time to drive to all the major mining sites today," he said. "Some other day, you might want to check out Irwin and up around Spring Creek Reservoir."

The first stop on the "tour" was Gothic, where a portion of the old town remained only because the Rocky Mountain Biological Laboratory was there. Each summer, scores of scientists and students lived in primitive, arthritic cabins in order to study the richest display of wildflowers in the United States. In winter, the few hardy souls who chose to remain were snowed in until the spring thaw. The only way in or out of Gothic in the winter, Dan informed the group, was by ski or snowmobile.

"What was life like here?" Mr. Rappaport asked, and Lana tried to muster up some enthusiasm and interest for this day-long adventure that carried her farther and farther away from her goal.

"The streets were probably filled with burros, and tents and log cabins dotted the hills and gulches. There were plenty of saloons, numerous gambling establishments, even dance halls. In one of the dance halls, so I hear, the girls wore skirts just above the knees."

"Really!" Mr. Rappaport began to drool only seconds before his wife administered a swift jab to his ribs with her elbow.

"How do you know so much about all this, Dan?" Lana asked, a hint of natural journalistic suspicion creeping into her tone.

"Lana, it's hard to live up here for long without

knowing the history. You can't really separate what this area was from what it is now."

Lana took in the bald scrapes across the faces of some of the mountains surrounding them. "Well, *I* can certainly separate what it was from what it is. And it seems to me that today's mining corporations could learn a lesson from the early miners."

Dan glanced back in his rearview mirror, but refrained from commenting. John didn't refrain. He leaned toward Lana and whispered, "If you're referring to Ryan Resources and what it has done to the natural beauty of the mountains, you're absolutely right."

Surprised by the remark, she turned to ask him exactly what he meant, but John was already looking out his own window again. He had been thinking the same thing that Lana was. He had always been secretly ashamed of some of the mining industry's methods, but there had been very little he could do about it. At least until a couple of years ago. He had never had the courage to use his position in Congress to vote for land reforms and mining regulations the way he had wanted to. He owed so much to his family, and he wasn't going to publicly embarrass them by voting for laws that would specifically hurt their business. But almost two years ago, he had finally developed his own scam to relieve his guilty conscience without publicly humiliating his parents. He just hoped to hell his father never found out what he was doing!

Dan left Gothic, headed down through Crested Butte Mountain ski area, skirted the town of Crested Butte, took Jack's Cabin Cutoff, then followed the Taylor River toward Taylor Park and Tin Cup.

"Okay, Dan, let's have the history." Lana surprised herself with the request. Where did this sudden interest about this area come from? After all, she was simply "doing her time" today, putting in a show of interest to waylay Dan's suspicions. *Don't lose your focus, Lana. The subject here is John Ryan, not the history of Gunnison County, Colorado.*

Dan didn't show his surprise over her question, but he felt it all the same. He had been wondering about her lack of interest in the area since that was supposedly the reason she had come up here. But that too was beginning to gel in his mind. There was too much antagonism and electricity between John and her, and though John hadn't told him anything specific, Dan sensed a growing emotional link between the two of them.

"Okay," he answered after a substantial pause. "Let's see if I can get it straight. Somewhere around eighteen-sixty a grizzled prospector named Jim Taylor heard tales of gold and silver in this region, and he and three other men decided to take their chances with the Indians and cross the continental divide.''

"They must have made it since this is called Taylor Park," Mr. Fisch replied eruditely between shutter clicks.

"Yes, indeed," Dan said, never missing a beat. "Although I think at one point their horses were stampeded by bears and they were forced to walk the rest of the way. Oh, by the way, it's kind of interesting how the town of Tin Cup got its name. According to legend, Taylor scooped up some promising looking gravel from Willow Creek in a tin cup and, in the light of the campfire that night, realized it was full of gold."

Mrs. Rappaport thumbed through the history book in her lap. She had bought it in Gunnison and already had quoted from it at least ten times. She thumped on the back of his seat. "Oh, no, Mr. Granger, I'm afraid you're wrong. It says right here that the town was called Virginia City. It doesn't say anything about Tin Cup. Only Virginia City. See right here, Sidney? See, it says Virginia City."

Lana thumped the air behind Mrs. Rappaport's head, then leaned over to John and whispered. "What do you want to bet she's been waiting all morning to catch Dan in a flub?"

John rested an arm around Lana's shoulder and bent close to her ear, whispering. "Maybe if we're 'lucky, she'll fall in some open, abandoned mine shaft.''

"One where a bear and her cubs have made a home," Lana giggled.

John laughed. "You're a hard woman, Lana Munsinger."

"You're absolutely correct, Mrs. Rappaport." Dan recovered from the woman's criticism and smiled diplomatically. "However, what actually happened is that the town bureaucrats wanted the town called Virginia City, but the citizens finally forced a vote and changed it back to Tin Cup."

"Well it doesn't say that in the book, Mr. Granger. I'm looking right at it and it doesn't say that."

"Shut up, Agnes!" her husband commanded, and Lana slid down in her seat, holding her palm tightly over her mouth to deaden the sound of her laughter.

John cleared his throat to remove a chuckle. "From what I've read, those early miners really were fascinating characters."

"Courageous sons of gun anyway," Dan said. "Not only did they have to put up with the Ute Indians who were always on the rampage over white miners, but the winters were almost unbearable."

"How did they survive it?" Lana asked, once again peaked with interest despite her best intentions to remain detached from it all.

"Well, if they were smart, they moved some-where else during the winter. But a few die-hards did stay with their families, even though numbing temperatures were often thirty degrees below zero and snows were extremely heavy and deep."

Silence prevailed for a few golden moments, until a growl from Lana's stomach intruded into the scene. "I don't mean to complain, but if we're going to talk about adversity . . . is anybody but me hungry?"

They stopped the truck along Willow Creek and unloaded the picnic basket and thermoses. Mr. Fisch sat on the tailgate reloading his camera while Mr. and Mrs. Rappaport dug through the basket, grabbing two sandwiches each. John reached into the basket and brought out two sandwiches, hold-ing one of them out to Lana. "Come with me."

Lana stared up at the incisive lines of his jaw and nose and mouth, into the quietly probing depths of his brown eyes, and all will and purity of thought left her mind. All she wanted in that mo-ment was to be in the circle of his arms, her heart pounding in syncopation with his, her mouth once again knowing his sweet plunder.

Her hand slowly lifted and took the sandwich from him, and following his lead she walked si-lently with him to the edge of the water. John sat down on the grass, reclining on an elbow, and Lana leaned against a large boulder beside him.

Tender aspen trees rippled in the early afternoon breeze above their heads and the water flowed confidently downward on its journey to the valleys far below. A few birds cackled in a nearby pine and time seemed to float by on a placid current of quiet reverie. They were both caught for several minutes in its ebb and flow, their own very private thoughts trapped in the downward pull of the stream.

Where the sun struck Lana's hair, ash-blonde strands glinted like rivulets of gold. The top two buttons of her flannel shirt were open and John became aware of a small blue vein that traveled around the curve of her neck, disappearing beneath the collar of her shirt. In his mind, he reached out and traced its path down into the space between her breasts.

He forced his gaze toward the creek. "Did you always want to be a journalist?" he asked, trying to ignore the rustle of desire that shook deep within his gut. Keep it light, John. Focus on something besides that pale neck and that tempting vein.

"I never really thought about it much," she shrugged, taking a bite of her sandwich. "It was what I was born to do."

"Are you kidding me?"

Lana caught the quizzical tilt of John's head. "No." How could she expect him to understand? How could anyone understand the genetic pressure that dominated her life? "It's just that my father, my grandfather, and my great-grandfather were all famous journalists, and since I didn't have any brothers to follow in their illustrious footsteps, I felt a kind of obligation."

John noticed that she was beginning to play nervously with her sandwich and with the plastic bag that had been around it, and he frowned.

"Don't get me wrong," she quickly inserted, shoving the half-eaten sandwich back into the bag. Her appetite was suddenly gone. "I love what I do."

John heard the tremulous quake in her voice, a kind of desperation that quivered in her words and gave a hard luster to her eyes. The look frightened him more than he cared to admit.

"What about you?" she asked too abruptly, wanting to close off the inner workings of Lana Munsinger from his probing thoughts. She didn't want him to see the doubt that crouched in a dark corner of her life, forcing its presence upon her now and then and pushing her to question her own goals. "How did you get started in politics?"

John finished the rest of his sandwich and stuck the empty plastic bag in his shirt pocket. "I was born to do it," he intoned solemnly, stepping to the edge of the creek and cupping his hands in the water to get a drink.

Lana stared at the strong back that was turned toward her, making a subconscious note of muscles that competed with the more sedate image of statesman and lawmaker. "You're going to get trichinosis," she snapped, hurt by the sarcastic echo of her own remark coming from him.

"Trichinosis!" he scoffed, standing and walking toward her. "I doubt that very seriously."

"Well, something. I read somewhere that you can get all sorts of diseases from mountain streams, from the animals that drink in them and—"

John was standing over her now, his hands flat on the boulder barely touching each side of her hips as he leaned down. "I've been drinking this water since I was a kid, Lana. Don't try to reform me at this stage of my life."

"I wouldn't dream of it," she retorted, trying not to stare at the chest that loomed so close to her, at the lean length of body that seemed to beckon her with every breath. "And don't give me that...you know what about being born into politics. Your father is a mining magnate, a far cry from a bureaucrat like yourself."

"A bureaucrat, am I?" His eyes smiled with deep amusement and he moved his face even closer to hers. Her breath was caught like a trapped bird in her throat and she could feel the blood in her veins bounding with eager anticipation. "Actually," he continued, seemingly oblivious of the effect he was having on her, "the truth is, it was there."

"What was there?" she whispered, then cleared her throat and tried again. "What was there?"

"Politics. It was suggested to me by a family friend—by the governor actually. It was there if I wanted it, readily at hand, along with everything else in my life," he added with a touch of cynicism. "So I took it."

His mouth was only inches from hers and she was aware with painful clarity that her body leaned toward him. "You just ... took it?

"Took it," he whispered as his mouth found hers, his tongue immediately tracing the full line of her lower lip, then moving like the silky flow of the river along the upper rim.

She heard a low moan and realized it came from within herself, and she grasped his neck with her hands as he pulled her up and into his embrace. Oblivious of the curious stares of Dan, the Rappaports, and Mr. Fisch, who were all less than fifty yards away, John's hands tunneled into the curling mass of hair and his lips moved in an urgent caress from her mouth to her eyes and then across her cheek.

"Your hair," he whispered huskily. "These beautiful curls ... why do you have them?"

She kissed the lower line of his jaw and her lips slipped to the inside edge of his shirt. "Oh, I just stick my finger in a light socket every morning." Her breath was featherlight against his collarbone and he tightened the grip of his arms around her. "John?"

"Yes?" His answer rustled like the breeze through the top of her hair.

"I'm not writing the story about Abscam." The minute the words were out, Lana felt an immediate sigh in the muscles of his body.

He stepped back, holding her at arm's length. "Really?"

"Yes. I checked it out and"—she looked up at him with a puzzled expression—"you didn't lie to me."

"I'll never lie to you, Lana. Never."

She opened her mouth to speak, to tell him that she was going to Denver tomorrow to get a story from his ex-wife, but the words would not come out. She was lying to him by not telling him. Guilt by omission. But she could not make herself divulge the whole truth.

John was aware of the tightening in her body, the cold fear that crawled by inches along her skin, transferring its message to his hands. There was more to all of this than Lana was saying, but what and how much he couldn't even imagine. But he was positive that she was holding something back.

He wanted to talk about this, get to the bottom of it, but the others were already packing up the wagon, so he reluctantly released Lana's arms.

There was still an awkwardness between John and Lana as the truck rumbled down the road toward Tin Cup, but it had a different complexion now. Back beside the creek, they had crossed some invisible line from which there was no return. They had admitted without words how much they had wanted each other. Their gestures had said it all. They had broken down the physical barrier. Now all that remained was the emotional one, but that would be the most difficult one to climb. Could they cross it at all? And if so, what would it do to the tightly woven tapestry of their very separate lives?

"How much do you already know about Tin Cup, Lana?" Dan asked, as he glanced back at her through the rearview mirror, still surprised by what he had seen between John and her at the river.

"Me? Nothing! Well... hardly anything." she stumbled over her words, falling into the trap set by her own lies.

"I thought since you were researching the family background maybe you might have some of your great-grandfather's records."

"No, nothing. I wish we did. All we know is that he went up into Pearl Pass to meet a mining company representative who had come over from Aspen. And before he reached the man, he was killed by Utes. If my grandfather knew anything more about his father's death, he didn't pass it on to us."

"You know, you might check in Crested Butte. There are some real old-timers who live there. Not old enough to have known your great-grandfather personally, of course. But his son... let's see, that would be your grandfather. He was editor of the paper there, wasn't he?"

"Yes, he was," she mused. A synapse of faint curiosity awakened in her, passing a sharp electrical current of interest through the neurons of her body, and for the first time in her life she wondered about just what kind of man Samuel Munsinger might have been.

She begrudgingly admitted to a certain growing regard for the area and its history as Dan continued relating the saga of Tin Cup. "It was a wild town, so I've heard. Violent and explosive. The Black Hills Gang controlled the mining camp and owned every marshal the town had. I believe there was only one lawman who wouldn't kowtow to them."

"Sounds like my job battling the Democrats in Washington," John boasted, somewhat out of character.

"The problem was, he quickly met with an unfortunate accident," Dan added.

Lana looked at John and lifted the corner of her mouth in a superior incline, but the smile quickly faded when his hand closed over hers. Her heart was pounding like the charge of the light brigade in her chest as she continued to stare at him, and the torch of unquestionable desire in his eyes inflamed the already heated core of her body.

"Do you think we can get away from the others for a little while?" John whispered, his breath striking her ear and sending a current of fire down her neck.

"Yes, please." She formed the words on her lips, but the sound dissipated when his hand closed over her thigh and his thumb began to stroke a slow rhythmical pattern through the denim of her jeans.

As they pulled into Tin Cup, Lana tried to focus her attention on the remnants of the town. Anywhere but on John's hand resting so possessively on her thigh.

There were quite a few structures remaining, certainly more than she had expected. An old church, its siding painted white, was in remarkably good condition and now served as the town hall. Several houses remained standing, as well as a portion of an old hotel. But it was almost unimaginable to think that it had once been a thriving city with a school, post office, several hotels, stores, and saloons.

Dan pulled the jeep to the side of the road so that they could get out and walk around. John helped Lana out of the truck and the two of them started walking through what was left of long ago hopes and ambitions.

Mr. Fisch snapped pictures, capturing silent, weed-covered ruins from every angle, and Mrs. Rappaport read aloud from her travel history guide.

"I'd love to know about some of the women

who chose to live up here." Lana peeked through an open doorway of a small log cabin.

"There were more than the normal number of ladies of the evening," Dan said as he walked up behind them. "And from all I've read, they were real characters."

"Normal number?" John laughed. "What is that supposed to mean?"

"Hush, I want to hear about them," Lana said, playfully striking his chest to shut him up. But John grabbed her hand, lifted it to his mouth and kissed the soft flesh of her palm and wrist.

Dan cleared his throat self-consciously at the outward display of affection between the two. This was certainly a surprise. John Ryan and a reporter. He sure never expected to see that happen. "One of the top madams was named Santa Fe Moll," he said, putting to rest this intriguing new turn of events in the life of his friend, John Ryan. "She got that name because she had worked the Santa Fe Trail years before. Then there was Tin Can Laura who made change for her customers from a tin can in her room. Wishbone Mabel... aren't these great names?"

"I'm almost afraid to ask this in mixed company," John grimaced. "But why was she called Wishbone?"

"Because of her bowed legs, of course."

"Ah, of course," he laughed, relieved at the simplicity of Dan's explanation.

"I see you have certainly committed these names to memory, haven't you Dan?" Lana teased.

"Well, Lana, an old man has to have his fantasies. Surely you wouldn't deny me that."

"I wouldn't dream of it," she smirked. "Any more names we should know about?"

"Yeah, there was Sagebrush Annie, who got her name from the condition of her hair."

"Oh, dear," Lana mumbled and automatically ran her fingers through her hair, trying to establish some order to the curls.

"They didn't have electricity back then, so I guess she didn't stick her finger in a light socket," John quipped, wrapping his arms around her and pulling her up against him.

Dan scuffed nervously at the dirt with his feet and actually blushed. "Well," he cleared his throat officiously. "Guess I'll go check on the Rappaports. And poor Mr. Fisch needs a mule train to carry all that camera equipment."

"Okay," John murmured, his undivided attention focused on Lana's lips. "I think I'll stay right here and feed some of my own fantasies for a few minutes."

A wave of undulating heat swelled in Lana's lower abdomen where it rested so intimately against John's. She could feel the warmth and solidity of his body and when his head lowered, she welcomed the bruising intensity of his lips on hers.

He finally released her, but she did not feel free. She knew somehow that her senses would never again break through the web he had spun around her. They would always be his to do with what he wanted. To provoke, to ignite, to fill.

She knew that this could never work between them. They were too different and their lives were on divergent paths. It would simply be too difficult to bring those roads together. And yet she stood there silently with her hair whipping about her face in the wind and passion rising in her like some long-forgotten dream, and her eyes pleaded with him to find a way.

# Chapter Six

"What I'd give right now for a time machine!" Lana held John's hand and with the other carefully pushed open a rickety door to look inside what must have been part of a lumber mill at one time. Along with this burning, new-found intimacy that flowed between John and her like gold down a narrow sluice, some latent curiosity, similar to that which must have stirred in her great-grandfather, had taken hold of her and she found her interest in this town growing by the minute.

"Some physicists have a theory that all time exists on the same plane, and it's only the limitation of our brains that forces us to perceive only one time line. What do you think?"

"I think you're way over my head," Lana laughed. "I just know that it would be nice if we could go back and see what it was really like for someone like my great-grandfather, wouldn't it?"

"We could pretend that we lived here," John

suggested pulling her into the old building for another kiss.

Lana placed the palms of her hands flat against his chest and studied him very carefully. "Hmm, yes, I think you would have been one of those crooked marshals, under the thumb of that gang— Black Hills, was it?"

John arched an eyebrow, then narrowed his eyes on her in deep speculation. "And you, my curly-headed angel, would have been the most heavenly delight in the local cat-house. Truly a high-classed lady of the night. You see"—he clasped her hips with his large hands, spreading his legs so that she fit in the crook of his thighs— "I would come to arrest you for some heinous crime of passion, but you would appeal to my kind heart, throwing yourself at my feet and begging me to spare you. And, being the soft touch that I am, I would give you one more chance to redeem yourself. Then you of course, overcome with gratitude for my largess, would shower every square inch of my body with kisses and plead with me to stay the night in your arms, saving you from further ruin."

Lana pursed her lips in annoyance. "Dream on, Marshal Ryan," she drawled seductively. "But the truth of the matter is, if you had come to arrest me, I probably would have taken my Hawkins rifle and put a hole clean through ya."

His mouth dipped down to her ear, his breath

warm and enticing against her skin. "I like my fantasy better. It sounds much more ... satisfying. Your warm, eager body under mine."

Lana's pulse raced with the husky sounds of his voice grazing sensuously along her neck. Her hands moved up the expanse of his chest, curved over the tops of his shoulders and wound into his hair in an unspoken invitation for what he so eloquently could give her.

When their lips met once again, John knew that, this time, Lana had surrendered her senses to him and would not ask for them back again. He pulled his mouth away and began to caress her face with his eyes and hand. His left hand slipped beneath the tail of her shirt and began to glide up the smooth expanse of her back. His thumb stroked beneath her arm and reached around to graze the side of her breast.

A murmur of excited voices broke into the hypnotic spell John's seductive wizardry had cast upon her and they both turned to the door as the voices grew nearer. They both sighed wistfully. He kissed her lightly on the forehead. "Guess we'd better join the others."

Stepping out into the bright light, the old town looked different somehow—golden in the glow of the sun, alive with the presence of dreams that would never really die. Hopes for happiness, plans for the future. Birth, love, laughter, tears, death. Inevitable processes of life that never changed or grew obsolete. Where once there was a thriving city full of men, women, and children who worked and played, cooked and cleaned, and tried to survive the long grueling winters, now there were only shrunken remnants among the wildflowers and weeds, and scattered along the hills were old whipsaw pits, rotting sluices, and overgrown prospect holes. But all was not lost. Because the dreams would never die.

Lana walked over to Dan who was kneeling in the grass, with Mr. Fisch and the Rappaports hovering over him.

"What is it?"

"It's some sort of tool. This area is so picked over for mining artifacts, I really didn't expect to find anything."

Dan handed it to Lana and she turned it over several times, staring with wonder. The minute she felt the cold metal in her hands, it was as if she were holding a part of her great-grandfather's life in her grasp. He had always just been an interesting character in her lineage. But now, suddenly, he was more. Holding this rusty, long-forgotten piece of equipment between her fingers, she was thrust back to the late nineteenth century when he was here. In her mind she could see him, hear him, reach out and touch him. She could imagine him talking to miners and townspeople, seeking out a story, his inquisitive mind always looking for a lead and a hook.

Lana looked around at what was left of the town. She took note of the tall mountains that surrounded it, and she had the strangest sensation that she had been here before, that she had been a part of the struggle that took place here in the late nineteenth century. Was John right? Did all of time exist in the here and now, or was Samuel Munsinger's experience in the mountains as ingrained in her genetic structure as the inquisitive impulse that had brought her here today?

"The old cemetery is down that road," Dan said, pointing to a vague spot among the tall grass to the west. "If anyone wants to walk down there ... I don't think the truck will make it."

"I'm staying right here," Agnes said. "You too, Sidney. If you go traipsing off, you'll get lost for sure."

"I think I'll wait here too," agreed Mr. Fisch.

"Okay," Dan said, resigned to staying behind with his guests. "John, we'll wait for you if you and Lana want to take a look. It's an interesting graveyard. This is the only place I've heard of in the American West where one could be buried in a segregated cemetery. The graveyard was divided into four knolls—Catholic, Protestant, Jewish, and boot hill burials."

"This I've got to see," Lana laughed. "Boot hill, really?"

"Keep in mind the outlaws were as much a part of the society here as anybody else. Half the popu-

lation carried guns. Most of the men wore big re-
volvers and belts of cartridges. There were even a
few two-gun men, but I doubt if many people tan-
gled with them. You never knew when they'd
shoot first and ask questions later.''

"Sounds like some reporters I know," John
murmured sarcastically, but with a teasing glint in
his eyes, as he and Lana headed down the road
toward the cemetery.

"Better than some politicians who duck and
hide behind issues with a lot of vague mum-
bling," Lana retaliated.

"Ah, yes, but you must remember, a mumble
cannot be quoted."

"Oh, yeah?" Her chin jutted out defiantly.
"We'll just see about that."

The hike took longer than they thought it would.
The cemetery was located about three-quarters of
a mile from town, near a small lake and the old
Tin Cup dump. Only about ten wooden grave
markers were left, most of them tilted at odd
angles from the years of erosion and by the heavy
weight of snow that cloaked the graves year after
year.

"It amazes me that I wasn't more interested in
all of this before," Lana sighed, stepping carefully
through the tall grass.

"I take it that is the reason you gave Dan for
coming to the lodge in the first place."

Lana was squatting in the grass, brushing away some dirt from a tombstone. She didn't answer, but her sheepish expression answered the question for him.

They each continued to study the various graves, holding back tall grass to read the names.

"Lana?" She looked up to see a strange expression on John's face. "Your great-grandfather's name was Samuel Munsinger?"

"Yes," she answered, a clammy chill inching its way up her spine.

"I think you'd better take a look at this."

She stood, but it felt as if her heart had stopped beating for several seconds and her feet didn't want to move. In a kind of daze, Lana walked over to John's side and stared down at the crooked wooden slab with the epitaph carved so precisely in its face. She knelt and brushed at the dirt that clung to its cracks.

Samuel Munsinger
Born May 10, 1843. Died December 8, 1881
I have fought my battle and lost,
but the truth will never die.

Lana stared for a long time at the grave, a vague quiver of foreboding clamping like a vise around her bones. Fought my battle and lost? The truth will never die? What on earth did that mean?

A light breeze lifted the heavy strands of hair

from her forehead and with it came another disquieting thought. She hadn't been in a cemetery since Tom's death and the contrast of the two burials now struck her as painfully jarring. Tom's parents had wanted him buried in Arlington, a hero's funeral—although Lana was sure that Tom would have preferred something with a little less pomp and severity. Certainly something less military. But his parents had wanted it that way and Lana had been in no emotional shape to debate them on it. The U.S. Marines had paid for her air ticket to Washington, D.C., and awarded her the respect of any hero's widow. Even the flag that had draped her husband's coffin was carefully folded by the honor guard and laid gently in her hands.

The words on Samuel Munsinger's grave faded to a blur as Lana's eyes began to burn. She shed silent tears for a man she wished she had known. And tears for Tom who should be buried here instead of in those meticulously manicured grounds where a wildflower or blade of grass that dared to make its presence known would be plucked mercilessly by an efficient groundskeeper.

"Lana?" John knelt down beside her, his head tilted at a quizzical angle and his forehead creased with consternation. He touched the back of her hair, letting his fingers glide down the curling strands in a gentle caress. "What is it?"

She shook her head and turned her face away

from him. What could she possibly tell him? She wasn't even sure herself what had caused the tears to fall. So much had happened to her in the last two days, her emotions twisted and wrung until all the juices of self-control were depleted. She had been attacked by too many remembrances of the past, memories of Tom that had been invoked and re-worked, sensations of desire and love for a man she had only known for two days and whose career she had come to plunder. And now this. Today she had found a piece of her great-grandfather's life, a solid link in the human chain that made Lana Munsinger who and what she was.

John touched her chin, turning her face toward him. He pulled her closer and kissed her gently, comforting her from a pain he could not see.

He pulled his head back and Lana offered a ten-tative smile. When he slowly wiped the tears away with the tip of his finger, she felt a love and grati-tude she had never known in her life.

"I didn't mean to cry," she whispered apolo-getically.

"It's okay." He plucked a white columbine from the ground by his knee and held it out to her. Her eyes closed briefly when his lips touched her fingers as they clutched the stem.

"I owe you an explanation."

"You don't owe me anything, Lana."

"It's so difficult to explain."

"Emotions always are."

Lana sighed, tilting her head back and letting the cool mountain breeze brush across her face. "This is the first time I've been in a cemetery since my husband died."

The hand that was resting against her back lost all feeling. A creeping numbness spread across his skin as the words sunk in. Husband? His eyes were glued on her face and he couldn't make himself look away. He had asked himself the inevitable questions—if there were any special men in her life, if there had ever been any. But a husband! For some reason that thought had never entered his mind. "When did he...?"

"Die? It's okay, you can say the word. I've had a lot of years to heal most of the wounds. It was eleven years ago. Vietnam. You know, one of those freak accidents that the military recruiters always forget to remind you of."

"You must have been very young."

"I was barely twenty." Lana absently traced the lettering on Samuel's headstone. "It was such a waste, John. Such a stupid waste of a human life."

John ran his hand down her arm and his fingers closed around her clutched fist. "The good in him, the friends he made, the people that he touched... like you, Lana. That wasn't a waste."

Lana watched John closely as he spoke, and she realized fully for the first time what a remarkable man he was.

"You must miss him very much."

"Yes." She smiled softly. "Sometimes I do. Tom was a wonderful boy." She paused over the memories. "Before he was drafted, he had great visions of being a foreign correspondent. To be honest, I'm not sure I could have been the type of wife to tag behind him all over the world, but...I would give anything to bring him back alive."

"I know you would." His eyes were soft and kind and understanding as he looked down at her, and she knew in that moment that she loved John Ryan. Whether she wanted to or not was beside the point. She did and she sensed that she could get very used to needing him in her life.

His fingers rested on her neck and his thumb stroked lightly along her jaw. "You know, I promised myself I wouldn't become involved with you. I didn't want to become serious about anyone. My own marriage ended in a death of sorts. It killed—or at least I thought it had killed—what little emotion was left in me. But with you I have feelings that I didn't even know existed. I have to be honest, it scares the hell out of me."

Lana watched his face for the truth and she saw it plainly written there. "It scares me too, John. But it's there all the same"

John lifted Lana to her feet, holding her at arm's length. Standing over the grave of Samuel Munsinger, the air pregnant with the scent of wildflowers and the summer breeze sweeping down in a stirring caress from the mountain tops, emotions that had been buried far too long in both of them were finally born anew. John smiled. "Then what on earth are we fighting it for?"

"It was at Garden of the Gods," Lana took a sip of her drink and smiled through the window of the bar out over the valley that lay below them. They had arrived back at the lodge less than an hour ago and the sun had already made its descent beyond the far mountains. "I remember it perfectly," she continued. "I was probably ten or eleven, I don't know. But I kept thinking that this was it, this was what it was all about. Being with a family, doing the simple things together." She looked embarrassed, hastily downing the rest of her drink. "Not a very ambitious thought, I know. Just something I think about a lot. You know, one of those crazy things that seems to sum up your childhood."

John reached across the table for her hand, and let his thumb stroke along the back of her palm as he held her fingers between his. "Yeah, I do know. Mine was in Canada. I was at summer camp . . . you know, one of those places where you fish and ride horses and take the wooden slats out of your counselor's bed."

Lana smiled and threaded her fingers between his.

"Anyway, there was this one kid that everybody just really hated."

"There always is one."

"I know, but in this case I just couldn't figure out why. He really was a nice kid. Not too straight, not too wild. Kind of middle-of-the-road. And everybody absolutely hated him."

"So what happened?" Lana asked.

John was frowning as he thought back on the years so long ago. "Well, it's really strange. He used to go off every day about dusk. Nobody could ever figure out where he went. Several guys tried to follow him at different times, but he always managed to lose them. So one day, I decided to go out into the woods ahead of him. I knew he always went in this direction, so I just waited for him. He didn't know I was there and I managed to follow him undetected. He came to this clearing and he pulled out a plastic bag from his pocket, then began tossing what looked like bread crumbs all over the ground."

"Food for an animal, maybe?"

"I think so. But he saw me. He turned around and had the most horrified look on his face. Then he dropped the bag and ran back down through the trees to camp. After that, he never went off at dusk again. He became as wild and crazy as all the other kids and everybody suddenly liked him." John stopped and stared into his drink. "You know, I've always had the feeling that I destroyed something for that kid. Something really valuable. He had a secret, a private place he went, and I invaded it somehow." John looked up at Lana and smiled, but it was introspective and somewhat wistful.

"He could have found another place," Lana insisted.

"Yeah, but you see that wasn't the point. Somehow, my finding his secret changed him. He wasn't the same person any more at all. He was just like everybody else." John suddenly grinned and lifted Lana's hand to his lips. "It really is crazy what you remember, isn't it?"

She wanted to answer, to say something to make him feel better about the still painful childhood memory, but at the touch of his lips against her palm, all coherent thought was lost. She stared at his mouth, wanting to feel it not only on her hand, but against her lips and body, whispering in her ear. Her gaze lifted to his eyes and she saw that he was watching her steadily, and his chest was rising and falling more rapidly than before.

"I'm sorry you lost your story about me, Lana."

She closed her eyes briefly, a shaft of guilt wedging into her thoughts. She should tell him about her plans for tomorrow, but... what would he do if she told him?

"Maybe we should go upstairs," he whispered with a sensual smile. "And I could give you a story."

Lana grinned, looking dubious but tempted.

"You know." He smiled, stroking the side of her face with his hand. "It's one of those private things . . . skeletons in the closet and all that."

"And do I need my tape recorder?" She turned her head slightly to kiss his fingers.

One corner of his mouth lifted slowly. "Well, actually, I hadn't planned on saying a lot."

"Sounds like a most enlightening interview."

"Oh, I promise you, it will be that." John stood and helped Lana with her chair, and the whole way up the stairs he secretly prayed that no one would stop their progress to his room. Relieved when they made it, he unlocked the door and Lana entered, standing awkwardly just inside the room.

John smiled at her and tossed his key on the bedside table. He walked back over to her, tilting her head up until she was forced to look at him. "You okay?"

She nodded, her voice stuck in the confines of her throat.

He watched her for a minute, then stepped away, opening the french doors to let in the gentle night breeze. "Have you tried the hot tub in your room?"

"No. I hate the things."

"You're kidding!"

"No, I'm not." She finally moved from the spot to which she had been rooted for the last two minutes. "If I want to sweat, I'll go to a gym. I don't like to just sit and sweat. I have to be doing something."

John smiled crookedly and Lana felt a flush creep up her neck and face. She looked away self-consciously, but she heard him turn on the jets. When she looked up, he was closing in on her, and she was aware of a substantial rise in her pulse rate.

"Come on, get in with me. You're going to love it. I'll make sure you have something to do." His mouth opened over hers and the mineral rich glide of his tongue along her lipline stirred the golden fires of need within her.

He pulled back and stood before her lifting his hands to her blouse, his fingers resting on the top button. His eyes drilled into her, looking through the depths of hers into the soul that lay beneath, waiting to be conquered. "Yes?"

She nodded again, unable to find the words to deny him anything he wanted. She felt as if her body were devoid of sensation except in the tips of her breasts and deep inside her abdomen. As if he knew those were the only points of her body that existed right now, the only ones that mattered.

Her eyelids dropped shut when she felt the first button slip through its hole, followed immediately by all the others. John pulled open her shirt, and she caught the surprised but pleased flicker in his eyes when he realized she was wearing nothing under it. He seemed spellbound by the rhythmic rise and fall of her breasts as he watched her lift her arm and unhook the buttons at the cuffs, pulling the shirt off her arms and dropping it on the floor at their feet.

He quickly unfastened his own shirt and pulled her to him, his large hand roaming across the bare back that felt so incredibly soft to the touch.

She inhaled sharply when her breasts first touched his chest, the sensation of skin against skin so electrifying she could only cling to him for support.

John lifted the hair at the side of her neck and bent his head, pressing his lips to the spot he had exposed. His mouth moved slowly upward, resting near her ear. "The tub is probably very hot by now. I promise you it will be nice, Lana." His teeth lightly gripped the lobe of her ear, and she pressed her lower body into his.

"I know." She longed for the touch of his body in a way she had never felt about a man before. This was new, different, totally encompassing. She watched in fascination as he peeled his shirt off the rest of the way, then unclasped the belt on his jeans and slowly pulled it through the belt loops. It dropped soundlessly on the shirt that lay at his feet. He reached out to unsnap the waistband of Lana's jeans, then slipped his hands inside and around the curve of her hips, kneading the bare flesh as he pulled her against him.

John's mouth closed over hers, devastating in its fiery intensity, his tongue plunging into the depths of her mouth while she responded by curving her body into him. His hand moved between them, fingers slipping into the warm space that subtly arched closer for his touch.

His tongue was now circling her lips, following the same motion as his hand and a low moan was wrenched impulsively from her throat. When his fingers stopped, she had the inexplicable urge to grab his wrist and force him to continue working his magic on her.

His hand moved upward, palm flat across her abdomen. He looked into her glazed eyes and a tiny smile tugged at the corners of his mouth while he pulled her jeans slowly down, easing her out of her clothes before stepping back. He stared at her for a long minute, his gaze moving by microscopic degrees across every curve of her body. And she watched him too, the way he breathed, the broad expanse of his chest, the smooth, flat plane of his stomach as he let his own jeans drop to the floor.

He took her hand and led her to the deck where the cold air raised tiny goose bumps all across her body. Stepping into the tub first, he held both of her arms and guided her into the water with him. The water was hot as they eased down into it, contrasting sharply with the cool air on their faces. But soon the heat rose around them enclosing them in a warm cocoon of steam.

"I thought it would feel colder than it does," she said when John laid his palm against her cheek.

"It's nice, isn't it? So private, yet so open and free. I like being part of the night."

The cold white moon was just lifting over the rise of the mountains, but as they watched it, it climbed rapidly into the night sky. Soon its reflection was mirrored in the lake below, a solitary orb of light that enlarged in concentric circles when the breeze skimmed across the water's surface, ever enlarging until the wind moved on and the circle was left intact and solitary once again.

"It should be another nice day tomorrow." John sat down and pulled Lana onto his lap, facing him. He held her tightly against him while jets of hot water massaged every square inch of their bodies.

"How do you know?" Lana asked, clasping her hands around the back of his neck and closing her eyes as he kissed her throat. "Were you really a weatherman in the Air Force?"

"Absolutely," he breathed against the skin of her neck, trailing his tongue upward to her ear. "Weather forecaster."

"Is that so?" She pulled her head back, looking at him seriously while he traced the familiar blue vein in her neck with his finger. He stopped only inches above her breast and she froze, waiting breathlessly for him to continue his descent.

"Would you like a lesson in meteorology?" His finger slowly circled her nipple and her breath was finally expelled into a vaporous cloud of desire.

"Oh, yes," she sighed. "By all means."

He leaned forward, tracing the line of her lips once more. "Well, to begin with," he whispered against her mouth, "when two very different air masses meet, they do not ordinarily mix."

"No?"

"No. That is not unless their temperatures"—his hands closed over both breasts and his thumbs were stroking the tips—"pressures, and relative humidities happen to be very similar."

"Yes, I see what you mean," she responded in a husky whisper. "Tell me more."

John's hands were stilled as he silently watched her. Finally, he stood her in front of him and slowly ran his hands the length of her torso. The water was hitting her just below the waist, but she felt no chill. Her body was on fire from the heat his hands created by their touch. "Such a willing pupil." He smiled, touching the peak of her breast with his tongue. He moved to the other breast, pulling it into his mouth and she grasped his hair, bending her head over him.

He let go of her breast and ran his hands down

her hips and the back of her thighs. "Sometimes when a front moves in, the change in properties and characteristics of one air mass to those of another is very gradual." His hands eased between her thighs, searching, pulsating, kneading. "At other times, it is quite abrupt." His fingers entered her body in a maddening quest for buried treasure, and she felt her body's own abrupt changes taking place within her. A low pressure center was forming inside her, growing stronger, rising in waves of passion and heat that lifted her to heights of exquisite rapture. She could feel his fingers over her, around her, inside her. She was consumed by his large hands and she wanted to consume every part of him.

John's mouth began a long, slow, foray across her torso, his tongue trailing fire and ice down her stomach to the slight swell of her lower abdomen where the water began. She bent over him, her hair falling over her face and onto his back. His mouth moved back up her body and when it reached her neck, he lifted her in his arms and carried her from the tub.

Their bodies moist and warm, he lay her across the bed and nestled his own body in the intimate spread of hers. Lana ran her hands up his chest and over the tops of his shoulders, circling the back of his head with her fingers.

"I was going to tell you all about an occlusion," he whispered, finding it more difficult to speak every minute. "But I think we're already there."

"I think you're right," she sighed, parting her lips to welcome the invading hunger of his tongue at the same moment she felt the warm, sliding sensation of his body as it entered hers. Her body was forced aloft, higher and higher, until its identity was lost in the upper reaches of the atmosphere.

Outside the open doors, the moon hovered above the lake in witness to their undulating fusion. And while the warm air caressed their entwined bodies, they were swept helplessly into the center of a raging storm of passion.

Lana was aware of nothing for a long time. Finally, she felt the warmth of John's hand as it glided slowly and gently from her hair all the way down her side. He smiled when she opened her eyes, but she noticed that his own eyes were still enveloped in the fog of yearning. He touched her cheek gently. "Cold?"

"I don't know," she answered truthfully, her mind and body not yet a part of the world of reality.

John lifted her up and pulled the bedspread back, laying her between the sheets, and pulling the blanket up over both of them. Propped up on one elbow, his hand trailed leisurely down her body, retracing the still sensitive hollows.

"That was some interview," she sighed, closing her eyes as her body began to react once more to the magic of his fingers. "There's only one problem," she moaned, aware of the undeniable heat building within her again.

"What's that?" He pulled the blanket back and bent over her, tracing the tip of her breast with his tongue.

"Since I didn't get to tape it...." She stopped, her voice and all conscious thought lost in a haze of wild sensation as he moved lower, letting his tongue glide down the warm expanse of her abdomen.

"Yes?" he whispered against her thigh.

"I might need to go over a few points again."

Her whispered words barely reached his ears, but he looked up at her and smiled. "My thoughts exactly."

As their bodies once again melded together in a storm of passion, they were carried across a thousand universes into that place in space and time where they were swallowed by the night.

For Lana, tomorrow and all that it might encompass were a million light-years away.

## Chapter Seven

The laugh that emanated from the woman's throat was hideous and cruel. "You must be kidding, my dear." Anne Ryan poured herself a drink and then walked back to the couch. "The man doesn't have the balls to do anything about it. Figuratively speaking, his family cut them off at birth, didn't you know?" Again she made that harsh, grating sound that was more spiteful than a laugh could ever be.

Lana closed her eyes against the blinding pain that enveloped her. Why had she done this? Why had she come here? She thought of early this morning, when she woke up in the circle of John's arms.

"Why do you have to go to Denver?" he had asked, startled when she first told him.

"I have to see my editor, John. There's...a meeting. I can't miss it." She hated herself for every lie she told him, but she couldn't stand the

/

thought of what he might do if he knew she was going to see his ex-wife.

"Will you come back?"

"Yes. Tonight or tomorrow at the latest."

He had rolled over on top of her. "Is everything okay, Lana?"

"I love you, John."

Lana felt a surge of nausea attack her midsection as she listened to the woman on the couch across from her. It was all she could do to forcefully restrain from slapping her arrogant face. She hadn't liked her from the minute she met her. Anne Ryan was one cold woman.

She was of medium height, with a good build, and platinum blond hair that was sleeked back from her face and fastened in a tight, meticulous bun at the back of her head. She had ambitious green eyes, a sadistic mouth, and cold chiseled features that might even be described as classically beautiful. Clinical, Lana quickly decided after meeting her. The woman belonged in a hermetically sealed jar.

They were sitting in Anne's suite at the Hyatt and a stack of dust jackets from her new book lay conspicuously on the table between them. Her explosive novel, *The Washington Wife,* was expected to be, if not a great literary achievement, a tremendous commercial success.

"The senator has groveled at his father's feet for so many years," she continued, "he wouldn't

know how to make his own decision about anything."

*His name is John, you bitch. John.* "Did you
know about his involvement in any F.B.I. investi-
gations?" *Stay calm, Lana. Calm, cool, and col-
lected.*

"The senator never informed me of his little
activities, curricular or extra." Anne took a sip of
her drink and watched Lana over the rim of her
glass. What was this woman after anyway? Anne's
eyes narrowed on Lana, petulantly wondering
why the focus of this interview had turned toward
the senator instead of on her new book where it
should be. "Would you like a copy of my publicity
photo?"

Lana smiled ingratiatingly. "Sure. Do you have
any idea what your ex-husband's feelings are
about running for president?"

Anne sighed. This conversation was becoming
tedious at best. "If I really thought the senator
had any chance of reaching the White House, I
would have stuck it out with him. That, my dear,
is where I want to be."

"Why?"

"Why!" Anne Ryan's beautiful face crinkled
with impatience. "Read my book, Miss Munsinger. I have spent the best years of my life striving for a position in that town. I pushed that man
and worked my tail off trying to help him get
where I thought he wanted to go. But he doesn't

give a damn about the presidency. He doesn't even really care about the Congress."

"Then why did he—"

"I threw lavish dinner parties, Miss Munsinger, entertained all the right people, planted seeds of tainted innuendo at the right places about his opponents. I did it all."

"For him?"

Anne looked baffled for a moment. "For whom?"

"John."

"Did I do it for John? John Ryan?" Anne's eyes grew wide and then she burst into uncontrollable laughter, holding her sides, and wiping tears from her eyes. "I did it for me, Miss Munsinger. Me! The senator was my ticket to where I wanted to go. If it hadn't been for me, he would have been some rinky-dink lawyer in Boulder or Colorado Springs. But I made him someone. A newsmaker. An important figure in this country. I was important. I was the princess of Washington society, and I only had a little farther to go." Her eyes glittered with hunger. "I was almost there. I was almost queen."

Silence permeated the air of the hotel suite. Lana was too stunned to respond and Anne was lost in her own bitter world of unfulfilled ambitions.

The eldest daughter of a famous playwright, she'd had a long string of "mothers." Of course, she rarely had contact with any of them since her formative years had been spent in boarding schools in France and Switzerland. When she'd returned to the States at eighteen, she had been one of the most sought-after debutantes in the country.

Boring rapidly with it all, Anne Bouchard had set her sights toward another horizon. She had money. She had looks. And she had all the friends her money and looks could buy. But she had wanted more. She wanted power.

When she was introduced to John Ryan, an up-and-coming politician from Denver, she took the dive. He had all the right attributes to move quickly up the ladder. And with her at his side, they would move to the top where she would be known and respected throughout the world.

"He told me he wasn't going to run." Anne's voice now drifted aimlessly like a lost chord. "After all the years I had worked for it, he wasn't going to run."

"Why do you suppose he decided not to run?" Lana was getting bored with Anne's self-interested narrative. She wanted to get to the meat of the story, something significant about John. And the fact that he wasn't going to run for president was fairly significant. But was Anne right? Did he have no intentions of running, or was it simply an excuse to get rid of a wife who had used him for fifteen years?"

Anne looked up at Lana, her mouth held in a brittle line. "He doesn't care about any of it. He never did. He said I pushed him. William Hartison, then the governor of Colorado, supposedly pushed him. His financial backers pushed him. He told me he'd always hated it. Said he wished everyone had left him alone so he could have practiced law like he had wanted to do in the first place. Told me all he wanted was a house in the mountains and a small law practice down in a little hick town somewhere. Can you imagine that? Me in the mountains!"

I can imagine pushing you off a mountain. Lana smiled sweetly, but her mind was buzzing with diabolical fantasies of what she would like to do to Anne Ryan.

Anne was unaware of the sadisic gleam in Lana's eyes as she continued ruminating about her cruel fate. "And in the last couple of years, he has become so obsessed with that land acquisition scheme of his...."

Lana's ears perked up like an inquisitive hound's. "Land acquisition?"

"You've heard of Voz de la Tierra?"

"Of course," Lana said. Everyone in Colorado knew of that organization. Voice of the Earth. It had sprung up a couple of years ago as a secret fraternity of wealthy entrepreneurs who bought large chunks of available land with the express purpose of turning it into wilderness areas for the state.

Though its membership roster had remained a closely guarded secret, the goals of the organization had captured the minds and hearts of the people of Colorado. A people's crusade to save their own land from the exploitation of mining conglomerates and commercial enterprise.

"You mean John is a member?" Lana asked, startled by this bit of information.

Anne smiled slyly, pleased with herself for having possession of such highly guarded information. "I have other names too." She reeled off several unfamiliar names and one that Lana did recognize. Dan Granger. Dan and John were both members of Voz de la Tierra. Incredible!

"And do you know what they're doing with that land, Miss Munsinger?"

"Buying it for donation to the state," Lana shrugged. That was common knowledge. Nothing new.

But Anne Ryan sat smugly secure on the couch and shook her head.

"No?" Lana asked, bewildered by Anne's gesture.

"One night, I was going through his desk... looking for something of mine, of course."

"Of course."

"I ran across some papers for Tierra, and attached to them were notes on Ryan Resources, listing some parcels of land the corporation was trying to buy. Those parcels are the ones that Tierra ended up buying.''

"Maybe Tierra was trying to buy them out from under Ryan Resources," Lana suggested, aware with every passing second of a tightening in her chest.

"Miss Munsinger." Anne drew out the syllables with precision, as if she were speaking to a child. "You're a reporter. Surely you understand the senator's difficulties of being a public figure and the son of one of the most powerful mining magnates in the country. He is under constant scrutiny. He can't publicly help his family's business while in office. Anything he does to help them has to be under the table, if you know what I mean."

"Are you saying that Voz de la Tierra is a front for Ryan Resources?" Lana was incredulous. It couldn't be!

Anne's smile was full of spite. "You know none of the land has been turned over yet to the state for those wilderness areas. I'm telling you, Miss Munsinger, John Ryan is using Tierra to buy land cheaply for his family's mining operations, land that wouldn't be sold to Ryan Resources if they made a bid for it."

Lana started to ask another question, but Anne Ryan stood and walked to the door, opening it for

Lana to leave. "I'm afraid I don't have any more time today. I have a talk show to tape in less than an hour and I have to get ready. I hope you'll excuse me now."

Lana looked at the woman who had been John's wife for so many years, and she felt a piercing shaft of pain slice through her body. "Thank you for your time, Mrs. Ryan."

"Good day, Miss Munsinger." Anne Ryan closed the door and leaned her back against it. She had just found the key to her revenge. John and his precious Tierra. She was going to destroy him and his plans the way he had destroyed hers. Her mouth twisted into a devious smile and she had to forcefully restrain herself from laughing out loud.

"So what are you going to do?" Dan cast his fly into the water.

"About what?" John pulled his fishing pole back and then, with a flick of his wrist, sent the line slicing through the air so that the fly landed on top of the water.

"About your life." Dan kept his voice low so they wouldn't scare the fish. "That is what this two-week furlough is all about, isn't it?"

John moved to another spot a few feet away and recast his fly into the stream. They had taken the jeep along a four-wheel drive trail, following Cinnamon Creek to a spot where Dan had fished before. He claimed it to be one of the best fishing holes in the Elk Mountains. And Dan Granger had probably fished enough of them to know.

He was right, too. They had already caught five rainbow trout between them.

"I'm not sure if I want to run for reelection or not." John's voice was low, but it carried easily to Dan through the quiet, thin air.

"Why not?" It didn't really surprise Dan. Nothing did. But he wouldn't accept the statement until he knew the reason.

"You're going to think I'm nuts when I tell you," John smiled.

"Try me."

"Okay, you asked for it." John paused for several seconds before speaking again. "It's not fun."

Dan's gaze flicked to John for a quick second before moving back to the water. He pulled his pole back slowly and tossed the line back into the water. Even with one arm, he was a damned good fisherman. It had taken years of practice to learn how to hold the pole under his right arm and use his hand to pull up the line with a fish on it. But he had learned and now it was second nature to him.

"Who told you life was supposed to be fun?"

"No one. I figured that one out all by myself."

Dan's reply was a vague nod. He was busy watching the water. He saw the fish swim toward the fly, felt the familiar tug on the end of his line, then grasped the pole in his armpit and jerked on the line with his hand until the fish was caught on the hook. Wading to the bank, he held the slippery fish under his chin while he removed the hook, then dropped him in the bag with the rest of the catch.

John wasn't watching Dan wrestle with the fish, for his mind was elsewhere. The sky was perfectly clear today and there was a light breeze that cooled the back of his neck. He gazed around at the towering landscape, at the green carpet of grass that surrounded the creek. The breeze whispered through the pine trees and blew the heady fragrance through the air.

He wished Lana were here. Wished he could lie with her in the warm grass. Together they could fill their senses with the beauty around them. They could smell the pine trees, listen to the gentle rush of the creek, watch the birds circling lazily above. And they could make love.

It had been exceedingly difficult to think about anything else since last night. He kept seeing her face under him, the glaze of passion in her eyes, the light blue vein in her neck that tempted his lips time and time again. The feel of her fingers closing around him, the pulsating warmth of her body as he lay buried deep within her. God, he hoped she'd come back soon!

Dan had slipped another fly onto the end of his line and was back in the creek again. "So, what made you suddenly get the crazy notion that life was supposed to be fun?" Dan smiled, already knowing the answer before he even asked the question. "Couldn't possibly have anything to do with that little Munsinger gal, could it?"

John grinned. He felt more like he was eighteen than forty. But damn, he missed her! "She's special."

"I figured that. Is that the only reason you don't want to stay in politics?"

"No, I'm not sure she's the reason at all. Hell, with her, it might even be fun." John paused as he thought about what a life in Washington would be like with Lana. Certainly different than with Anne. But he really didn't want a life of politics for either of them.

"No, you know I've been thinking about retiring for a couple of years. I'm tired, Dan. Tired of the dynamic inaction in Congress, tired of the backscratching and the backstabbing. I'm just plain tired of that city. I've decided that Congress is just a big daycare center for those of us who have reached our level of incompetence. The people don't know what to do with us so they elect us to Congress. Most of the time our sessions are about as productive as a morning in a daycare. We argue, we shout, we lay blame on the opposite party. We fuzzify the issues and study the problems so long, they finally just fade away."

"Fuzzify?"

John laughed. "Lana taught me that one."

"Figures."

"I don't know, Dan. I just seem to have lost the focus, if there ever was any. When I was on the armed services committee, we'd pull in generals from the Pentagon and never know if they were plying us with the same misinformation they fed to the Soviets. When I was on the Senate Ethics Committee, we slapped the proverbial wrists of congressmen who had used the office for less than ethical purposes. When I look back to add up the things we've actually accomplished... well, let's just say it's bleak as hell."

Dan shrugged. "It serves a purpose."

John shook his head as if in disagreement. "Maybe it's because the job has been so lacking in challenge from the beginning. I've never really had to work for the position. My campaign managers and backers did all the work. As they say, if you don't have anything to do, do it with style. And that's exactly what I did. All I had to do was smile and look charismatic and the voters, my campaign manager assured me, would flock to the polls to see me elected."

John dropped the tip of his fishing pole into the water, his mind drifting along another track entirely now. "I took the easy road, Dan. That's the problem."

"Are you feeling guilty about that?"

John thought about it for a minute before shaking his head. "Bored, I think."

"So Lana Munsinger is a fun-filled diversion, a relief from your boredom. Is that it?"

John's head jerked up to glare at the other man. "No!" he spoke emphatically. His thoughts toward his friend softened when he realized Dan had merely been trying to make him think about just how much she meant in his life. He smiled as he remembered the way she felt last night curled up beside him in bed. "No, Dan. She's a new beginning."

At Almont, Lana kept to the left on Highway 135 toward Crested Butte. She'd had the radio on blaring all the way from Denver, trying to drown out the agitated thoughts in her mind. She was angry and she didn't know what she was going to do about it. She wasn't even sure at whom she was the most angry. Was it John, or was it herself? Or maybe it was simply the situation.

Her mind was a jumble of contradictions, mazes, and puzzles, and she couldn't make the pieces fit together or find a way out of the trap. She loved John Ryan. She knew that last night, and she still knew it. But she did not love what he stood for, and she wasn't sure she could bridge that gap in their relationship.

Now that she had met Anne Ryan, Lana could easily understand John's cynicism toward love. How he had managed to live with that woman for as long as he had was beyond her. But this business with Tierra, this was what she couldn't deal with. How could he do it? And Dan too! How could they abuse the public's trust this way?

Voz de la Tierra had come to stand for so much in this state. And its secrecy had only added to its appeal. But what would that same public think when they learned what was really being done with their land? That a few greedy men were buying it up as cheaply as possible, only to turn it over to those who would destroy it.

She and John had even talked the other day about the irrevocable damage the mines had done to the mountains, the irreparable scars. And he had agreed with her. And yet now he was buying up more land to turn over to his family's mining business. He had duped her. He'd led her to believe he could do nothing wrong, nothing illegal. He had charmed her the same way he had charmed voters for years.

Defrauding the people of this state. That's what John Ryan was doing. The man she loved was a fraud.

Well, she was a reporter, first and foremost. And she could not sit on a piece of information like this without reporting it. She loved John and she didn't want to hurt him, but at the same time she cared about this state and the people had a right to know what was happening to their land.

By the time she pulled into Crested Butte, it was

nine o'clock, and she didn't feel like she should call the lodge to send someone to get her at this hour of the night. Besides, she wasn't sure she could face John right now anyway. She had to think this thing through before she saw him again. And in all truth, she wanted to find a couple of those old-timers Dan had mentioned and perhaps learn a little more about her grandfather's and great-grandfather's lives.

She drove down Elk Avenue and parked in front of the historic Forest Queen hotel. It wasn't much to look at, but if it could provide her with a nice soft bed, that's all she cared about right now. It had been a very long, exhausting day and a good night's sleep was in order.

After checking into her small clean room, Lana walked to the Eldorado Cafe and ordered a hamburger. Sitting on the balcony and lingering over her meal in the glow of a lighted lamp on her table, she began jotting notes on a legal-sized pad of paper. She listed all the major points she wanted to cover in the article. Succinct and to the point. That was her style and that was the way Walt liked them. No editorializing. Just state the facts and let the public read between the lines.

Her pen poised in stop-action above the paper, and a wave of revulsion undulated through her. What was she doing? How could she do this to John? She loved him! She wanted her story, yes. And she wanted the fraudulent land acquisition scheme stopped. But she didn't want to ruin John's career.

In her mind, she could almost hear the scolding of her father, grandfather, and great-grandfather over her hesitation. You're a journalist, Lana, they were saying. You're a Munsinger! This is your job in life. Your destiny.

Slowly, Lana's pen began to move once more upon the paper. By the time she stopped writing, she had filled several pages and the article had come to life. She cupped her hands over her eyes to soothe the strain in them from working under such dim lighting.

She cut and edited and reworked and when she once again read the article objectively, she knew that it was good. Walter Finch would be proud of her. Her father would be proud of her. She closed her eyes again, trying to conjure up a feeling of pride for herself. But there was only contempt for herself over what she had done. It carried with her into her sleep that night breeding in her mind and haunting her dreams.

## Chapter Eight

John walked downstairs to breakfast, feeling as giddy and highstrung as a libidinous adolescent. Lana would probably be here sometime this morning and his blood was already bounding through his veins in anticipation of the moment when he would see her again.

He sat down at his favorite table and studied the menu, finally deciding on sausage, biscuits, and gravy. The waiter took his order and turned to walk away. "Oh, by the way," John halted the young man's progress toward the kitchen. "I didn't get my newspaper this morning. Could you bring me one please?"

The waiter nodded noncommittally, and walked away, leaving John frowning in his wake. He shrugged and sipped at his coffee. The paper was always outside the door of his room each morning and he was very surprised not to see it there this morning. Dan's staff was phenomenal about those kinds of details and he probably would not be very happy to know that there had been an oversight. But John wouldn't say anything about it. No one had a legitimate complaint about the service in this lodge.

When John looked up again, he saw Dan walking toward him with the newspaper under his arm. He was wearing a very strange expression and John wanted to immediately put him at ease. "Don't worry, Dan. It was a simple oversight. I didn't really need the paper until now anyway."

Unsmiling, Dan sat down across from him without responding and without handing the paper to John. Finally he spoke. "I instructed my staff not to give you the paper, John."

"Why?" John's face clouded with official concern. "What's happened, Dan?"

"Nothing of international import," Dan quickly reassured. "I just don't like to see my guests upset and ... well I thought this might." He handed the paper to John who was frowning with confusion.

John opened the paper, quickly scanning the front page to see what might upset him.

"Page three," Dan said.

John turned the page and his eyes immediately landed on the photograph of his wife. She looked the same as she always had, immaculate and sterile, with her hair in that same perfect coif that she would never allow to be touched. There had been very few times that he'd even wanted to. There was nothing touchable about this woman and never had been.

His eyes dropped down to read the copy. She was in Denver, accepting interviews from every reporter and tabloid that showed any interest in her. She was publicizing her new book and the things she had to say about life with Senator John Ryan were far from flattering. The accusations and innuendos she alluded to on a local talk show could hurt his chances for reelection a lot. If he cared.

John looked up at Dan and shrugged. "I might as well get used to it. I know this won't be the last I hear from my dearly beloved ex-wife."

"It could really hurt you in the campaign, you know."

"I know. And you want to know something, Dan? I don't care. I've decided I'm definitely going to drop out of the race."

"When did you come to this decision?"

"Last night. For the first time in my life, I know what it feels like to be in love with a woman. To love her above all else. I want to ask her to marry me, Dan. And I can't remain in politics and be married to a journalist. It would just never work."

"So why can't she give up her career?"

"I don't really care about my career any more. All I ever wanted was to be a lawyer in a small town. I wanted that before and I still want it. And Lana needs her career more than I do."

"Maybe too much?"

"What's that supposed to mean?" John snapped, refusing to face any of the doubts that he, himself, had already felt on that point.

"How badly does she need her stories? Is she still writing one about you?"

"Lana loves me, Dan. She wouldn't do anything to affect our relationship."

"How do you know?"

"What is this, Twenty Questions?" John's voice dropped to a furious whisper. "You never have liked her or trusted her. I know that. We've been friends a long time, but you have no right to interfere in this."

Dan nodded his head slowly and turned to gaze out the window. "Call me a meddlesome old fool, John, and you'll be absolutely right. But I care about you. You're like a son to me, and I don't want to see you hurt anymore. I just want to ask you one question. You said Lana went to Denver to talk to her editor."

"Right. So?"

"So, why couldn't she call him on the phone from here?"

"Oh, for God's sake, Dan! How the hell should I know? I'm not going to analyze her every little move and you shouldn't either." John grimaced, not wanting to ask the question, but knowing he would anyway. He hesitated. "All right, so why do you think she went?"

Dan didn't answer, but his eyes involuntarily flicked to the newspaper on the table. John's eyes followed and landed on the photograph of Anne. His gaze jumped quickly back to Dan who was shaking his head sadly.

"I hope to hell I'm wrong, John. I really do."

After breakfast, Lana decided to have a look around Crested Butte. Though she wouldn't admit it to herself, she was avoiding going back to the lodge. She had already called the story in to Walt and he was, quite predictably, understated in his praise. But Lana could tell he liked the story and that at least for now her job was secure. But she felt no elation at having completed a job well done. A heavy weight seemed attached to her chest and she knew that it would not go away any time soon. So, instead of facing John, she decided to spend the morning searching out the old-timers here that Dan had talked about.

Settled in 1880, the town of Crested Butte still harbored its century-old Victorian flavor and was designated as a National Historic District by Congress in 1975. As Lana walked along Elk Avenue, she was able to absorb much of this historic flavor. Bars and restaurants with quaint names like The Wooden Nickel, Three Thieves, and The Water Wheel sported fresh coats of paint hiding the signs of age.

She passed the small office of the *Weekly Citi-*

*zen* and stopped. Turning around, she opened the door and walked in to the tiny office. Two women dressed in western shirts and faded jeans were typing away at desks too large for the small confines of the room. They both glanced up, revealing only slight interest, then one of them went back to work at her typewriter while the other one brusquely asked Lana what she needed.

"I was wondering if you knew anyone in town who lived here seventy or eighty years ago."

The woman's eyes narrowed on her for a moment and the one at the typewriter stopped working to stare. In the last ten or fifteen years, too much progress had been foisted upon this town. There was the ski resort just up the road, hundreds of plush condominiums, and a mining company venture that would bring in thousands of new people to process thirty thousand tons of ore each day. The townspeople—those who came in the sixties to get away from a society they no longer wanted to deal with—were wary, and possibly with good reason. They wanted things the way they were ten years ago and they couldn't yet accept that they would never be the same again.

Lana rushed ahead to explain. "You see, my grandfather used to be editor of this paper. Frederick Munsinger."

The women still watched her with blank eyes, although their shoulders had relaxed somewhat.

One of them finally smiled. "We didn't know him. That was before our time."

"Well, I just wanted to meet and talk to someone who might remember him. Better yet, someone who might have known him fairly well."

"Check out the thirteen bar stools at Kochevar's. At least ten of them will be Crested Butte natives. Look up a guy named Franrak. He'd probably know something."

"Yeah," the other said, "Or maybe...hey, didn't old Jack Stark work for the paper?"

"I think you're right. Then there's always Bessie Calhoun," she snickered as she jotted down a couple of names on a piece of paper and handed it to Lana. "You should be able to find these old cronies down at Kochevar's."

"Okay, what's the best time to catch them?"

One of the women checked her watch. "The bar opens at eleven." She smiled up at Lana. "You just made it."

Lana laughed. "I see. Thanks so much. I really appreciate it."

"Say, where are you staying?"

"Pine Lake Lodge."

"Oh." The women turned back to their work, erasing Lana from their minds in a split second.

Shrugging, Lana went out into the warm summer day. She walked down the sidewalk to Kochevar's and smiled as she noticed the outmoded sign in the window which read, "Ladies Welcome."

The only light in the bar came from the bare windows and her feet made a hollow, awkward sound as she walked across the floor. Only a couple of elderly men sat at the far end of the bar and the bartender, a young man whose hair was pulled back in a pony tail, wiped a cloth along the top of the white oak bar. The three men glanced up at her in passing interest then turned back to their former activities as she sat down on a stool.

"Hi." She smiled at the bartender.

He nodded in return. "Brew?"

"Yes, please."

"Coors? Oly?"

"Olympia will be fine. Thanks." Lana smiled again as she took a napkin and wrapped it around the icy bottle. She glanced down the bar at the two old men deep in conversation. They were both wearing overalls, flannel shirts and drab tractor hats. She consulted the piece of paper the woman at the *Weekly Citizen* had given her and then turned back to the bartender. "Do you know where I can find Jack Stark or Al Franrak?"

The two men at the end of the bar stopped talking and looked at Lana. The bartender cocked his head toward them and spoke out of the side of his mouth. "Stark, you've got a visitor."

Lana looked at the two men. "Is one of you Jack Stark?"

"I am." One old man removed his faded red hat, scratched the top of his head, then slipped the hat back on. His nose was red and bulbous, perhaps from too many years sitting on Kochevar's bar stools sipping brew, and the whites of his eyes were the color of yellow ochre.

Lana picked up her beer and strolled down to the end of the bar. "I'm Lana Munsinger. My grandfather was Frederick Munsinger. I wanted—"

"What'd she say?" Stark frowned like a man continually frustrated with trying to figure out what in tarnation the younger generation was talking about half the time. He looked to his friend for interpretation.

"She says Frederick Munsinger was her grandfather. Munsinger, you geezer, Munsinger."

"Well, I'll be dogged! If that don't beat all!" Jack Stark wiped his hand on his overalls then stuck it out to shake Lana's. "Munsy's grandkid. Well, I'll be dipped in molasses!"

Lana smiled and glanced quickly at the bartender who only shrugged in response. He was used to the old codgers and he also knew it took a circuitous route to get any information out of them.

"This here's Pittman," Stark said. "Joshua Pittman."

Lana shook hands with the other man and this time spoke slowly and distinctly. "I was wondering if I could ask you a few things about my grandfather."

"Who?"

"Frederick Munsinger . . . Munsy."

"Oh, sure. Let's move over here to a table."

For the next thirty minutes, the two men regaled Lana with stories of the past. Tales of hard work, frigid winters, mining treasures, and wild pranks that Stark and Munsy used to play on each other. They had obviously been good friends and Jack liked nothing more than reminiscing about the old days.

"But they weren't always good days." He pointed an unsteady finger at Lana to make sure she understood. He had no teeth on his lower jaw, and his bottom lip and chin tended to recede into his neck at times. "The Depression hit hard even up here. Mines closed down. People moved out." He shook his head, remembering. "Tough times. Yep, hard times."

He stopped shaking his head and suddenly grinned at Lana, revealing the gaps in his upper teeth. "But what a town this was! What a goldarn good time we had when Munsy was alive. Ain't I right, Josh?"

"Yep, you're right, Jack." Joshua Pittman figured he had put in his two cents' worth and then went back to work on his beer.

"Did he ever talk about his father much?" Lana asked, eager to get to the crux of the matter.

Jack was shaking his head again, grinning, his thoughts trapped in the maze of past days. "What was that?"

Lana sighed, trying to be patient. After all, someday she would be sitting where Jack Stark was now. Old, toothless, and probably senile. Oh Lord! "I was wondering if he ever talked about his father?"

"Who talked about his father?" Jack frowned as he tried to follow the conversation.

Joshua Pittman slammed his beer bottle to the table in exasperation. "Munsy, you old coot. She's talking about Munsy's father."

"Oh." Jack ruminated for a moment longer and Lana wondered if he'd forgotten what she asked him. "His papa was real famous around these parts," he said, and Lana heaved a sigh of relief.

"Did he ever say what Samuel was doing up here in the mountains? What kind of story he was working on?"

"Something big, I can tell you that."

"What do you mean?" Lana rested her forearms on the table and watched Jack with rapt attention. "What was it?"

"Munsy never knew for sure."

Joshua cleared his throat. "Your grandpa weren't much of a reporter."

Jack ignored the interruption and continued. "It had something to do with one of the mines outside Tin Cup. Whatever it was, it got him killed."

Lana frowned, trying to understand what Jack

Stark was talking about. Samuel Munsinger was killed by Indians. What would that have to do with a mine? She shrugged. "Yes, but as I understand it, the Utes often went on the rampage against white men up here."

Jack's lower lip was sucked back into the cavern of his mouth as he turned his age-rimmed eyes on her. "Weren't no Injuns, little lady. You can take my word on that."

Lana stared, the full impact of what he was saying not taking effect for several long seconds. "Are you saying...Samuel Munsinger wasn't killed by Indians?"

Jack made a smacking noise with his lips. Joshua Pittman sucked his beer and seemed oblivious of the whole thrust of the conversation. "Not Indians. Munsy was sure of that."

"But then who? Who would have had reason to kill him?"

"Munsy's papa found out something about one of them mines up there that either the government or the mining company or both didn't want him to know."

Joshua set his bottle of beer on the table and looked at Lana, joining the conversation for the first time in several minutes. "I wouldn't go stirring up that can of worms, if I were you." He glanced at Jack. "You know what happened to old Bessie?"

Lana's gaze jumped from one old man to the

other. Bessie. The women at the *Weekly Citizen* had mentioned someone named Bessie. But they had snickered as if it were some kind of joke. "Who's Bessie?"

Stark continued making loud noises with his lips and Pittman thoughtfully slurped his beer, both thinking back on years behind, days that were and people that are no more. It took a few long seconds before Jack responded. "Bessie Calhoun. She was Munsy's—" He looked to his friend for support, but finding none, turned back to Lana. "Your grandma didn't like it much up here. Too cold, too far away from everything. Finally she couldn't take it no more. So she took her boy—I guess that's your papa—she took him over to Denver to live when he was about twelve. She never came back. Munsy and Bessie became... real close."

"But the years have been hard on Bessie," Joshua inserted. "You won't get nothing out of her."

"You mean she lives here?" The bubble of excitement that had been expanding inside Lana was about to burst. This was what she had waited all her life for. This was the story she had trained for. This. Not a sensational piece of yellow journalism on a senator who, she realized now, had not even had a chance to deny her written accusation before she gave it to her editor as fact. No, this was the type of investigative story she had always dreamed of writing and now she had her chance. She wasn't going to lose this one. "Please, tell me where she lives."

"She lives up Deadman Gulch in an old cabin. But you won't get nothing out of her. She's crazier than a loon."

The information the two old men had given her was still being absorbed in her mind. But one point ran clear. Samuel Munsinger had not been killed by Indians, and she intended to find out exactly how he did die. "I'd like to try. How do I get there?"

John stood against the side of the lodge, leaning his weight into the log structure. He checked his watch for the hundredth time. The driver had left almost two hours ago to pick up Lana in Crested Butte. They would be here soon. He had spent the morning walking in the surrounding forests trying to make sense of his conversation with Dan. Maybe he should have known. Damn it, he had known. Even when she'd mentioned that she was going to Denver, he had known that she was not telling him the whole truth. It was the way she said it, the hesitation, the eyes that wouldn't look directly into his, the little things that spoke of some kind of deception.

He looked out over the valley and frowned. But Anne? Did she really need a story about him badly enough to go see his ex-wife? That wasn't journalism, that was muckraking. He slapped the log siding with the flat of his hand. But then maybe he was jumping to conclusions. She might have gone to see her editor. There could have been something that she couldn't discuss over the phone with him. Dan was probably wrong, John decided in a fit of blind hope.

Something stirred within him, the juices of desire, the tensing of muscles that expanded in anticipation of her arrival. He saw a flash of metal in the distance. The sun striking the blue frame of the four-wheel drive wagon. It was still a couple of miles away, and those last rough miles to the lodge were the slowest.

He would have to ask her, of course, but maybe the answer would be revealed in her eyes. She could step out of the jeep, run to him with eyes blazing with love and faithfulness, and he would know beyond a shadow of a doubt that she had not gone to see Anne. Yes, he would see the truth in her eyes.

And he would have to tell her that he was going to withdraw from the senatorial race. He had come to the decision last night and he was positive he was doing the right thing. He had spent too many years trying to please too many people and it was time he started pleasing himself. There was a house west of Denver that was for sale. He had already seen it, thought about buying it, just in case he decided not to run for

another term. It was a good price, was surrounded by trees and a small stream. It was just
what he had always wanted. And it was the perfect size for a family.

He shifted on his feet, scanning the horizon for
another glimpse of the truck as it inched its way
around and over the mountains.

His thoughts shifted back to his decision to
leave the political arena. He would have to tell his
father and mother. He didn't want them to read it
first in the newspaper. Maybe after he told them,
he could let Lana break the story. He closed his
eyes and took a deep breath. *Lana, please let me
find out that you were with your editor yesterday, not
with my ex-wife.*

He saw the truck make the last rise and descend toward the lake. It plowed through the far
end and the water sprayed in all directions from
the wheels. He took two more deep breaths, letting them out in quick puffs the way he always did
before a campaign speech or a press interview.
Breathe in, breathe out. The jeep was almost here.
He got his first glimpse of Lana as the truck pulled
into its parking space beside the lodge. She was
looking at him, but he couldn't make himself
smile. He couldn't seem to move a single muscle
in his body. He waited.

Lana saw John standing there before they even
pulled up to the lodge. The lone figure, insulated
in his solitude, was holding a silent vigil in his wait

for her return. She had played the reunion scene over and over in her mind on the drive up here. But she couldn't get it to come out quite right. What was going to happen when she told him where she'd been? And she did have to tell him, she knew that. Would he understand? Wouldn't he have to?

She wanted to smile at him, to raise her hand in greeting, but his solemn stance was too intimidating. It was almost as if he knew, or perhaps that was simply her conscience talking. Her hands remained in her lap and she watched him for any clue that he was happy to see her. She saw none.

She thanked the driver and stepped out of the truck. As she walked toward John, she thought she detected a hint of a smile lifting one corner of his mouth. That one encouraging sign gave her all the impetus she needed to run to him and throw her arms around his neck. "John," she cried, as her hands clutched his hair and she felt the first touch of his lips upon the bare skin of her neck.

When she threw her arms around him, every doubt in his mind was pushed farther back. Only the joy of seeing her again, and the need to hold her forever trumpeted forth in conscious thought. His arms held her tightly, squeezing and clinging at the same time. His mouth found her neck, the spot where he remembered that light blue vein began. She smelled so good and felt so soft.

Lana tilted her head back, her lips consciously

searching for his. When she found them, they were warm and demanding and worshiping. Her tongue immediately met his in the interior of his mouth and she felt the sum total of her existence centered in that one spot of contact.

"I missed you, Lana." He finally broke the union and breathed heavily into her neck.

"I missed you too, John. And I have so much to tell you." Did she imagine it, or did his body tense against hers?

He heard what she said, even knew what it meant, but he didn't really want to recognize it right now. He had been thinking about her too much the last couple of days. Now, he needed her body next to his. "Tell me about it in my room, okay?"

"Yes," she said against his shirt. "Yes."

They hurried into the lodge, hoping that nothing or no one would stop their ascent to satisfaction, and they both heaved deep sighs of relief when they made it to his room without interruption.

"John, there is so much I want to tell you about what I found out. I met these two old men in Crested Butte and—" John had closed the door and his hands were running over her body. She couldn't think when he was doing this to her. She didn't even remember what she was saying.

She leaned back against the wall and let his hands play their magic games across her breasts and waist and thighs. Her own hands were resting on the front of his shirt, but his fiery caresses had left her incapable of movement. Everywhere he touched her, a permanent impression was formed. His mark was made; it would stay with her forever. She closed her eyes and pulled at the material of his shirt, clutched it between her fingers until she felt it fall open. She felt her own blouse slipping from her shoulders, and he yanked it impatiently over her wrists.

As soon as her bra was unclasped and discarded, she was pulled against his chest. The feel of his skin against hers, the scent of his hunger pressed her toward him and pulled her pelvis upward into his.

"Every second of the last day and a half has been spent waiting for you, Lana. Don't leave like that again."

Her eyes squeezed tightly shut. How was she going to tell him that she had spent her time learning about his deceptive land acquisitions? "No, I won't," she whispered, clinging to him more tightly than before.

He lifted her, carried her to the soft spread upon the bed. Lying down with her, he wound his long fingers into the curling strands of her hair. He opened his mouth to ask her, wanted to find out if she was with Anne. But he couldn't. Instead his hands pulled hard on her hair and his mouth dropped down to her breasts, taking out his hunger and doubts on the soft peaks and inclines of her body.

Lana arched her body upward, silently begging for more of the punishing reward of his mouth. She knew she should have told him about Anne, somewhere in her mind the guilt registered, but her body refused to ignore the exquisite fire that spread rampant and out-of-control across her skin. She felt her nails rake along his back, paying him back for the painfully sweet torture he exacted on her.

His hands slipped into the waistband of her skirt, moving to the back where he deftly unfastened the button that held it in place. There was no patience and easy grace in the removal of it from her hips. It was wrenched from her body, in the same way he was wrenching her love and her soul. Taking, demanding, both of them wanting to punish the situation that gave so much deception and uncertainty to their relationship, and wanting to drive away any traces of doubt between them.

Without leaving the bed or her side, John removed the rest of his clothes then, wedging a knee between her waiting thighs, they came together in an explosive, unrestrained cataclysm, their bodies and their minds and their souls drowning in the utter bliss of physical binding.

Afterwards, John remained on top of her, his face buried in the moist warmth of her neck, Lana's fingers trailing langorously down his spine.

The violent storm of passion that had erupted between the two of them had passed and they were
both left in the wrecked aftermath of its fury.

Lana's hand lifted to the back of John's head.
She was afraid to look at his eyes, but she knew
she must. She had to talk to him about the last
two days.

John tried to keep the words from spilling from
his mouth, but he no longer had the buttress of
his driving sexual desires to hold them back. He
had to know. "How was Anne?" The words were
torn from his lips, running hot along the crook of
her neck.

Lana's hand stopped stroking John's head. She
did not breathe. She did not move. "What?" she
croaked. How could he have known? Was it that
apparent in her eyes?

John lifted his head finally and looked down at
her, his eyes dull and his mouth thin and tight.
The flinch in her body and the wide apprehension
in her eyes told him all he needed to know. And
yet he wanted to hear it from her own voice. He
clenched his jaw tightly before repeating the question. "I asked you how Anne was."

Lana stared back at him, devastated by the hard
pain that emanated from his eyes. "Fine," she
whispered. "She was . . . informative."

"I'm sure she was," he said dully, pushing
himself off her and sitting on the side of the bed,
massaging the back of his neck. He expelled a

long, weary breath. "Why, Lana? Why was this story that important to you?"

"My editor told me if I didn't have a story about you by this morning, that he would fire me."

John turned around and frowned. "Why?"

Lana sat up, but looked down at her hands clenching together repeatedly. "Because I didn't check out the facts before I came up here. I wasn't using responsible procedures to check out the story before spending the money and time to come here." She began to cry softly. "John, I love—"

John turned around sharply, glaring at her, daring her to tell him that she loved him after what she'd done. "So when does the story come out?"

"My editor is holding it until I get a statement from you."

"A statement from me!" John chuckled mirthlessly. "You really are something, Lana."

Lana tried to ignore the bitter tone that came from his voice. She had to get this over with. "I'm sure some people would say that what you're doing with Voz de la Tierra is fraudulent."

He frowned, confused by the statement.

"Buying land under the guise of ecological reform and then selling it at a profit to the highest bidder . . . or worse, giving it to your own family to mine . . . ."

"What have you done?" John's eyes were narrowed on her in a mixture of shock and threat.

"I think the question is, what have you done?" Lana countered with sarcasm, as she leaned over the side of the bed to reach for her clothes. "You're the one who's buying the land."

"And you think that I'm buying it to use for mining purposes?" John's jaw tightened ominously. "Lana, who knows about this—about me belonging to Tierra? Who did you tell? Does your editor know about this?"

Flustered by his brusque tone, Lana's eyes shifted nervously to her briefcase sitting on the table. John's gaze followed. He jumped up from the bed, stalking naked over to the briefcase where he reached inside and pulled out a stack of papers. Quickly scanning the papers, he closed his eyes briefly then stared hard at Lana. "You sent this to your editor?"

She nodded, tears once again forcing their way to the surface of her eyes.

He shook his head slowly. "You have no idea what you've done, Lana."

"What? Tell me!"

Ignoring her question, he quickly dressed, as did Lana, and began pacing the room, slapping the papers between his hands as he walked. "When is this going to run?"

"Not until I call my editor with—with a statement from you."

"You want a statement from me," he stated sarcastically, glaring at Lana, his eyes accusing and punishing. "I had no idea you wanted an exclusive so badly that you would resort to destroying my family, not to mention the damage this will do to Tierra. I suppose my darling ex-wife told you all of this." His jaw snapped in anger. "No doubt."

Lana was too stunned by his anger to even answer. John grasped her shoulders roughly and pushed her down on the bed, covering her frame with his own much heavier one. "You wanted an exclusive, didn't you, Lana?" he whispered venomously. "So why didn't you just write about what I'm like in bed. You seemed to enjoy that assignment so much. That sounds like the type of story you'd be best at."

Lana fought him wildly with her hands and arms, but he continued to pin her to the bed. But his anger traveled into her body in the wrong way. He made her want him again, long for him. At the same time, she wanted to slap his face for the horrible things he was saying to her. Things that she knew were absolutely true.

She began to cry, deep sobbing sounds that were wrenched from the bottom of her chest and John felt the hurt deep within his own body. Why had he said those things to her? But then, why had she written the story? He held her in his arms, stroking her hair and side with fingers that throbbed with the desire that was building in him.

He pushed himself away, slowly and reluctantly, afraid of his own reactions to her. He opened the closet door and stared for several seconds at the shirts and slacks hanging there. Finally, he pulled them out and, opening his suitcase, began to pack.

Lana dried her eyes and sat up in bed to watch him as he very carefully and patiently folded the shirts and then threw them haphazardly in a fit of frustration in the bag.

When she finally spoke, her voice was soft and tentative. "John, I'll call and...and cancel the story. My editor wasn't going to do anything with it until I called anyway. It's not worth this."

John threw his toothbrush and shaving kit into the suitcase and closed the lid, latching it tight. He straightened up and stared at Lana for a long painful moment. All he wanted was to crawl back into bed with her, to forget that any of this had happened. All he wanted was to love her and for her to love him. But there was more at stake here. She had a job to do, one that she would obviously not compromise for anyone, even him. It would have been lovely if it had worked out between them. But it didn't. He had to be realistic.

"Do whatever you want, Lana. It doesn't really matter any more. The damage has already been done."

As he picked up his suitcase and opened the door, looking back at her once more, Lana knew that he was not talking about damage to his career.

He was talking about what she had done to their relationship. To their love.

Like a piece of badly gouged marble on the verge of crumbling, Lana sat on the bed without moving, her blouse hanging open and her hair wild and unruly. Well, she had her story. Yes, she got what she had come here for.

Her head finally broke loose from the constraints her stunned emotions had held it in, and she let it fall forward onto her chest. Her story. The all-consuming, hard-driving need to have that one big scoop. Something to pin her name to as if that was what made her who she was. And now, she had done . . . what? The unpardonable? John had said she had no idea what she had done. He was right. She didn't know. And yet she knew that it had destroyed whatever love there was between the two of them. John was gone.

Lana climbed off the bed and walked slowly into John's bathroom. Turning on the hot water tap, she filled the claw foot tub with water and removed the rest of her clothes. After pouring in a capful of the fragrant oil that sat on the shelf above the bathtub, she climbed into the steaming mist, trying to wash away the layers of a guilt she supposedly should feel, but one she couldn't accept as entirely her own.

## Chapter Nine

Dan stood beside the lake, watching the glow from the setting sun as it lingered on the mountain tops. His right arm was in the pocket of his jeans and his stance was unflinching and straight. His face was cold and gray, like the hard rough bark of a pine tree in winter. From her position about ten feet away, Lana debated on the best course of action with him. *Straight on, Lana. Stop feeling so guilty about this. You're not the one who was wrong. He was. He and John and all the others who have duped the public with the supposedly benevolent activities of Voz de la Tierra.*

"Hello, Dan."

Dan turned set features upon her and nodded. He didn't smile and he didn't speak. Gone was all pretense to be the perfect host.

Lana swallowed hard then forged ahead. "Dan, I know you're a member of Tierra. I have other names too."

"So I've been told."

Ah, so John had already filled him in. Lana wondered what he had said, what he had disclosed to Dan that he would never tell her.

"Yes...well, then you must uderstand why I did what I had to do."

Dan's eyes widened for a split second and his mouth twisted in a smirk of disdain. "What you had to do! Do you have even the vaguest idea what you have done?"

"Yes." Her chin jutted forward and her words clicked out in a haughty, staccato beat. "I have exposed an organization—and its members—that has been defrauding the people of this state for the last two years." Lana shook her head in disbelief. "Dan, you have had the support of the people. Everyone has been behind this project because they believed that it was for them, for the state."

"And what makes you think it's not?"

"Anne Ryan explained to me that the sole purpose of the organization was as a profit-making scheme for its members."

"And you, of course, believed her."

"I had no reason not to."

Dan shook his head as he stared at her in bewilderment. "I knew the minute I met you that you were an ambitious woman. But I had no idea how far you would go and how irrational you could be."

Lana's head jerked. She was too stunned to even answer such an accusation.

"You had every reason not to believe Anne Ryan, Lana. But in your blind pursuit of a story, you refused to see that you were dealing with a deeply disturbed woman who is out to exact revenge on John in any form she can."

"Are you saying she lied?" Lana's tone was still haughty, but a thread of uncertainty wove through her words.

"I'm saying that Anne Ryan doesn't know, and never has known, what in the hell she was talking about. After several years of trying, John never involved Anne in his life in any more than a peripheral way. She doesn't know anything about Tierra. She doesn't know anything about John or what he stands for."

"What does he stand for, Dan?"

"It's a little late to be asking that question, don't you think?"

"I want to know," Lana answered seriously. "Please."

"John has spent the last five years in Congress walking a tightrope. Trying not to enact legislation that would hurt his family and friends and, at the same time, wanting to do what he thought was right for the people of Colorado and for the country as a whole. You have no idea how difficult that job can be, Lana. He owes so much to so many people. He has his financial backers to think of, his parents, and his conscience. He's just a man, Lana, and he didn't always make the right choices. But he did try."

"And if Anne Ryan didn't know what was going on with Tierra, what is going on?"

"Just exactly what the public thinks. Voz de la Tierra—or rather the members of it—had access to information about land that was for sale in this state. The membership had to remain a secret in order to retain that link to the information about the land. We heard about it before anyone else and were, therefore, able to grab it before those with mining interests got wind of it. And we made a lot of powerful enemies along the way. Ryan Resources and MinCorp just to name a few. Tierra had, and has, every intention of turning that land over to the state with the explicit instructions that it be designated as a wilderness area."

"But John's father owns Ryan Resources! You mean to tell me he is doing this behind his father's back? I thought he—"

"Loved his father? He does. Joseph and John Ryan have an extremely close father-son relationship. And Joseph has encouraged and supported John in everything he has ever done. But they have not always agreed on ideals. Sometimes John's conscience took him down a different road from his father. This is one of those cases. John has a great affinity for the land and how free and open spaces can enhance a man's life."

"So he joined Tierra," Lana stated dispiritedly.

"No, he created it."

"And he didn't want his father to find out."

Dan's mouth tightened at the corners and his eyes were washed gray. He turned back toward the treeline and did not answer for several moments. "Joseph Ryan is a very ill man. He can't take this kind of news right now." Lana thought back to that first night at the lodge when John had mentioned that there were other lives involved. He must have meant his father's. But his concern then was over Abscam. This... this was a deliberate attempt to undermine his father's business. Maybe that was what John meant when he told her she had no idea what she had done.

"I had no idea, Dan. I'll call my editor and cancel the story," Lana offered dejectedly. "He was waiting on a statement from John before he ran it anyway."

Dan pursed his lips and scowled at her. "A little late for that too, isn't it?"

Lana frowned, not understanding what he was talking about. "Dan, you have to understand. I never meant to hurt John... or you. I love him, Dan."

He turned away to stare out over the lake, but his words cut into her flesh like the cold blade of a dagger. "Every day we make decisions, Lana. We have to decide what is most important in our lives. You've made your decision."

"I did what I had to do! Can't you understand that?"

Dan looked at her long and hard. "Yes, I can understand that. I just hate the thought of what it has done to John. You see, he loved you too."

*Loved. Loved. He loved you too.* But no more. She had killed that love with ambition. "I'll call Walter and cancel the story and then I'll tell John." Lana was speaking out loud, but the words were no longer directed at Dan. She was trying to convince herself that all was not lost. That there still was a chance.

"John's on his way to Denver, Lana . . . to his father's."

"What?" she asked, the growing alarm draining all color from her face.

"I mean he left here immediately after . . . after he was with you. He wanted to tell his father before anything came out in the papers."

"But why? I told him nothing would run until I had a statement from him. Why would he do something so stupid?"

"You told him a lot of things," Dan shrugged. "He just didn't want Joseph to read it first in the papers."

"No! Dan, he can't do that. He just can't!"

Lana spun around and dashed through the lobby, taking the stairs two at a time to her room. No, she had to stop him. She couldn't let him do this!

As John steered his black Fiat up the winding, tree-lined driveway of his parents' home, the anxiety returned. He had been able to push it aside for a few hours while he made the drive from Crested Butte back to Denver. But now it was back. The proximity of the house and of the task at hand heated his palms until they were stuck like glue to the steering wheel. He had to do this. He had to explain it to his father before it came out in the papers. This lie he had been living, this fence he'd been riding, had to end.

As he neared the house, he noticed the sleek, silver Cadillac that belonged to the family physician. John's pulse beat faster. He hoped it was simply a routine call, the kind his father had become accustomed to over a year ago. Everyone knew he was a very sick man and didn't have much longer to live. John had accepted that, but he wasn't ready to face it. Not just yet.

His mother's gentle, worn face met John at the door. She smiled, tired but relieved to see him. And there was that spark—an acceptance and contentment that always seemed just under the surface of her eyes. "We were hoping you would get here, John."

A sense of panic gripped him. "What's happened? Is it Dad?"

She nodded and her eyes were a yellowed liquid, like iron that has been left too long in the rain. "He's bad, John. We tried to call you at Dan's, but he said you had already left. We could only hope that you were coming here."

"What happened? He was fine when I talked to him a couple of weeks ago. Is the doctor with him?"

Mrs. Ryan smiled wistfully and touched her son's shoulder. "Yes, the doctor is up there now. But he wants to see you. He's been asking for you all day. John, you've known that he couldn't last much longer. He's in so much pain."

John grasped her hand and held it tight as his mother began to cry.

"He's so tired, John. So tired." She leaned her head against John's chest and found comfort in the solidity and endurance of family ties. When her tears were spent, she stepped back and wiped the soft, loose skin of her cheeks.

John looked up the long, winding stairway and took a deep breath. "I'll go see him now."

"Yes." Mrs. Ryan nodded and walked from the foyer into the study, closing the heavy double doors behind her.

John stepped on the first stair and grasped the banister. Yes, he had known this moment was coming. But he had pushed the actuality of it into the far reaches of his mind. Always before he had been able to look at it objectively. It had been doctors' reports, biopsy results, treatments and procedures—never Joseph Ryan, the once-strong, seemingly invincible man who had stood as the tallest and most dominant force in John's life. Now, that's exactly who it was—his father, lying shrunken and defeated at last in the physical world.

John ran his hand along the varnished wood banister as he climbed to the top. He suddenly remembered the day so many years ago when he decided to slide down it and ended up on the marble floor below with a broken collarbone.

He turned and walked down the long hallway toward his father's bedroom. He passed several guest rooms and thought of the times when the house had been full of people. There had been the political fund-raising affairs, the business meetings under the guise of social extravaganza. There had been Christmases when he was young. The aunts, uncles, cousins, and family friends who stopped by with their presents and songs.

He reached the door to his parents' bedroom and slowly opened the door, a sense of dread at what he would find gripping him high in his chest.

The doctor was by the window, talking to the full-time nurse who kept watch over Joseph Ryan. They both looked up as John entered and the doctor appeared to heave a sigh of relief. "Hello, John," he whispered, patting his shoulder. "It's time to say your good-byes."

John glared at the doctor for one hostile, irrational moment before slowly nodding his head. The doctor and nurse walked out into the hallway and closed the door on John and his father.

They were alone. John looked over at the bed for the first time since entering the room. Joseph Ryan looked so small in the huge bed, almost like a young child with a very old face. His white hair was thin and sparse from the months of chemotherapy that had neither eradicated the malignancy nor mitigated the pain.

As John walked closer to the bed, he noticed a thin, dry smile on the older man's face and he couldn't help but return it. He pulled up a chair to the side of the bed and took his father's hand.

"Glad you could make it, son. Wouldn't seem like much of a send-off without you."

John cleared the suffocating lump from his throat. "Wouldn't miss it for the world," he quipped, but the light remark fell like lead from his mouth. "There are some things we need to talk about, Dad."

"Business to the end." He tried to joke, but his voice weakened at the last.

"Not business, Dad. It's about me. About what I've been doing with my life."

"You're withdrawing from the Senate race."

The voice was husky and labored, but a steady vein of tolerance ran through his words.

John's eyes widened in surprise. "How did you know?"

"You haven't been happy for some time," Joseph said. "I figured it was inevitable sooner or later. Do what you have to do, John. Don't worry about what other people expect of you."

John stared at his father for a long moment, wondering just how much he might know or suspect. Joseph had closed his eyes and his skin was pulled tight and too thin against the bones. "It's more than that, Dad. More than just withdrawing from the campaign."

The eyes flew open and Joseph smiled tiredly. "John, we've been father and son for forty years. There's very little I don't know about you. And what I don't know is your business. I love you. You love me. That's all that matters."

"It matters to me," John whispered, watching the sunlight dancing in the upper leaves of the tall oak beyond the window. "Hell, it's going to be in the papers tomorrow, so you'll know whether I tell you or not."

There was a long moment of reflection as father and son looked at each other, both knowing that for Joseph Ryan, tomorrow was an irrelevant term. "If it makes you feel better, son, you can tell me. But you and I both know it doesn't really matter now anyway."

John was silent for several minutes before he spoke. He was watching his father in a pose of sleep and he wondered if that slim space between life and death was in any way similar to that tiny moment between wakefulness and sleep when everything was so vividly clear, problems were solved, symphonies were composed, plays and novels written. Was it the same with death? Was that last lucid moment of existence the most creative and luminous, the most distinct and perfect?

"Dad, that organization that's been giving you and Ryan Resources so much hell for the last couple of years—Voz de la Tierra?"

The eyelids fluttered open and a quiet "yes" came from his mouth. But there was no expression in the haggard lines of his face.

John continued, reluctantly, painfully. 'That's me, Dad. I am Tierra."

The early morning sunlight drifted lazily into the open doors of her room, dancing along the tan planks of the floor and climbing by degrees up the flowered print wallpaper.

Lana folded her jeans and laid them in the bottom of her bag with her extra shoes and boots tucked around the edges. Occasionally she wiped away the tears that clung to her cheeks and replayed the scene with Walter over and over again in her mind. An unforeseeable snag in the system. That's what it had been. She had been sure that

Walt would understand that. These things just happened now and then.

*I think you need to grow up a little bit. Reevaluation. Better suited for something else.* His words. He had used them all last night and she was just now beginning to understand the truth behind them.

After she had left Dan, she'd come upstairs to call Walter at work. He was on deadline for the six o'clock edition and wasn't happy about the interruption in the first place. If she had thought about it more, she would have called him this morning when he was fresh. But she wanted to make sure the story was canceled. She couldn't let her own lies run in the morning edition. She had done enough damage to John already. All she hoped was that he had received her message.

She had tried to telephone him last night to tell him she had canceled the story, but his father's number was unlisted. Dan finally agreed to make the call for her, but he said that he was unable to talk to John or his mother. He had to leave a message with the housekeeper and Lana could only hope that the information would be passed on to him.

Thoughts of her conversation with Walter wedged into her consciousness again and a tear slipped from the corner of one eye.

"Where is the story on the senator?" he had asked, repeating Lana's own question. "Well, it's waiting for your statement from Ryan and any research backup you have. I'd like to run it in to-morrow morning's edition."

"Walt...you're going to have to kill the sto-ry." Lana had cringed at the silence that met her and she tried to prepare herself for the reprimand she knew she would receive.

"What?"

"The story about Tierra's land acquisitions... it was...false. Anne Ryan lied...or perhaps just didn't know the truth."

"Are you telling me that you sent in a story based on Anne Ryan's account alone? You had no backup? Lana, is that what you're saying?"

"I had no reason to doubt her account."

Walter Finch was silent for so long that Lana couldn't even begin to imagine what he might be thinking. "Lana, I'm not even going to waste my time telling you all the reasons you had to doubt a bitter ex-wife of a popular public figure or the re-sponsibility you or any other reporter has to sub-stantiate every claim, every accusation before it's printed. That's first-year journalism school, Lana. That's common sense. That's professional respon-sibility."

"You're absolutely right, Walter, and I—"

"Good, I'm glad you agree. Because you will surely understand why I'm telling you to pick up your final paycheck by tomorrow afternoon. Your things from your desk will be boxed up and set in the lobby at the security guard's station."

Lana's pulse bounded beneath her skin and every trace of color had drained from her face. Walter didn't really mean this. It was some sort of joke, an attempt to scare her into better performance. That's what it was. She had almost laughed at her editor's jest, but his next words stopped her cold.

"I think you need to do some reevaluation about where you're going, Lana. I think you need to grow up a little bit. You can't expect to live off the achievements of the other Munsingers. You have to achieve something yourself. You have to work for something. Maybe you'd be better suited for something else, some other line of work."

Lana haphazardly threw the remaining blouses in the suitcase and closed the lid. At the last minute, she remembered her toothbrush and tossed it in on top of everything else. She latched the bag and called the desk for someone to come pick it up.

Better suited for something else. There was the joke. What else was there? Journalism was her life. Without it, she was nothing. And yet because of it she had destroyed her own career and perhaps even the love of the most important person in her life.

She heard a rustling outside her room and flung open the door for the bellman to pick up her bag. But it was only the boy delivering the morning newspapers. She bent and picked it up, unfolding it to the front page. And there, emblazoned across the paper, was the black and white impact of what she had done.

### SECRET OF VOZ DE LA TIERRA UNEARTHED

The carefully guarded society of Colorado environmental philanthropists is under investigation by the United States Justice Department and the Federal Trade Commission because of accusations that U.S. Senator John Ryan, along with eight other members of the organization, was involved in the fraudulent purchase of public land.

The land was bought under the pretense of being used for public wilderness areas, but the question now being investigated is whether that land was purchased for the sole purpose of individual profiteering.

An official congressional investigation is also expected in the case of Senator John Ryan, in terms of possible violation of the Senate ethics code.

Lana backed into the room slowly and sat on the edge of the bed. When the bellman entered to pick up her suitcase, she stared through him with eyes that were glazed with shock.

She looked back down at the article. How could this be? This wasn't even the *Rocky Mountain News*. Anne Ryan must have given the same story to someone else. Lana groaned out loud. All she had done, all the trouble she had caused John and Dan... and herself. All for what? She hadn't even had an exclusive!

She turned the page to finish reading the article, growing sicker with every printed word that described the various parcels of land that Tierra had purchased over the past two years, land that was rich in valuable mineral deposits. ...

Republican Senator John Ryan was unavailable for comment due to the death of his father, Joseph Ryan, founder and president of Ryan Resources, a four billion dollar international mining conglomerate that extracts and produces every kind of mineral from uranium to molybdenum. A spokesman for the family would not reveal the details of the funeral, stating that Mr. Ryan's wish was for a private ceremony of family members only.

Every fiber of her being reacted to the death of Joseph Ryan. Because only Lana—and John— knew that she alone had caused the death of John's father. As surely as if she had plunged a dagger into his heart, she had killed the father of the man she loved. He had said, You have no idea what you've done, Lana. Well, now she did. She had probably ruined John's career and she had killed his father. And beyond a doubt, she had destroyed every shred of love that for a little while wove like a gossamer tapestry between the two of them.

All the things she'd worked for, all the dreams she'd ever had, simply slipped through her fingers like vapor and were gone.

## Chapter Ten

Mrs. Munsinger flipped the wall calendar over to
August and pushed the tack in securely to hold it.
"Lana, for goodness sakes, your father isn't some
two-headed ogre with green fangs." She turned
around, grabbing Lana by the shoulders and liter-
ally pushed her through the kitchen doorway into
the den.

"Yeah?" Lana mumbled. "Since when?" She
shuffled like a still rebellious seventeen-year-old
over to the chair where her father was reading the
evening paper. She stood in front of him for ten
long seconds—and she counted slowly—until he
looked up, grasping the bowl of his pipe with long
fingers. He puffed loudly several times, trying to
encourage the embers to reignite.

"Something you want, daughter?" He leaned
over to reach for his tin of tobacco and set it between his legs. Opening the can with a slim tool,

he dipped the pipe into the shredded, aromatic leaves and packed it full. Holding it between his teeth, he held a match to the bowl and drew noisily on the stem until it was lit and the smoke circled lazily about his head. He again looked at Lana over the tops of his bifocals, waiting for her answer.

Lana stuffed her hands into the back pockets of her jeans and shifted her weight to the other hip. *Get it over with, Lana. Go for it!* "It's about a job, Dad. I—I need one."

"Yes." He nodded slowly, puffing leisurely on the pipe stem. "I'd say you do."

Lana sighed and looked around the room restlessly. It had always been this way between them. He the celebrated idol on the altar, she prostrating herself before him. Who did she think she was kidding? She would never be his equal so there was no point in trying. He had been a figurehead in the family, someone to emulate, to revere, to worship from a distance. He always jetted off to some exotic locale to capture the local flavor in words. Or else he would sequester himself in the study and Lana and her mother would spend several days tiptoeing around the house and communicating by sign language. Now that she thought about it, life was much easier when he was away.

When Lana turned her attention back to him, she realized with dismay that he had been studying her. His head was wreathed in a cloud of smoke and his eyes were narrowed on her in deep speculation.

"Listen, if it's too much trouble, just forget it," she snapped. "I just thought that maybe you had a contact or — Forget it." She waved irritably and started to stalk off toward the door.

"Lana." Mr. Munsinger pulled the pipe from his mouth and set it in the ashtray.

She stopped, but didn't turn to face him. "Yes?"

"What are you doing right now?"

She turned and stared, confused by the question.

"I mean right now." he said. "Have you got an hour to spare?"

"Sure . . . I suppose." She shrugged, frowning in bewilderment.

"Good." Sam Munsinger laid his paper neatly on the floor at the foot of his chair and stood up, reaching for his pipe and a small pack of tobacco to stick in his shirt pocket. "Let's go get a beer."

If he had suggested she jump off the nearest bridge, she wouldn't have been more stunned. "Me? You want me to go get a beer . . . with you?"

"You do drink beer, don't you?"

"Yes, but—"

He was standing beside her now and he scowled down into her face. "When did you acquire a taste for it?'' he asked too gruffly, betraying a fatherly concern that touched her to the core.

Lana smiled for the first time since entering the room. "When I was seventeen. Let's see," she laughed. "I think you were in Peru covering the military coup at that point."

"Guess I missed a lot of momentous occasions in your life, didn't I?"

She looked up at him, seriously this time, but there was no malice in her reply, only a wistful sadness. "Yeah, you did."

The bar where he took her was small and derelict, the kind of place frequented by your typical ragtag league of journalists. Its decor was conspicuously unremarkable and the service was even worse. But right now Lana couldn't care less where they were. She was with her father. He had asked her out for a beer.

"So you want a job," Sam said, taking a long sip from his mug and looking every bit the celebrity still. "What kind of job?"

"I was hoping to get on with another paper. The *Denver Post* maybe."

"Not too conservative for your blood?" He smiled.

"Well, as they say, beggars can't be choosers."

"What happened to reduce you to the status of beggar?" Sam Munsinger was watching her steadily, reading character in the now tight lines around her mouth and eyes.

"Oh, it was really nothing." She brushed it off too casually.

"It's never nothing, daughter."

Lana sighed and took a long drink of her beer. "You're right. It was something." As she told him the story of what had happened at the lodge and with John, she kept watching his face for any signs of displeasure or censure. But there was nothing. He simply listened, keeping his thoughts carefully concealed beneath a bland expression that had come from long years of interviewing exceedingly dull politicians, grim dictators, and self-centered celebrities.

When she finished, he sat quietly, taking a drink now and then and she wondered, for a minute, if he had even heard her.

"Uh-huh," he finally murmured. "And what makes you think you're qualified for another job?"

Lana slammed her empty beer mug to the table in anger and started to rise. If she wanted verbal abuse, she could call Walter Finch. She certainly wasn't going to sit here and take it from her father.

Sam grabbed her wrist and pulled her back, forcing her to sit and glare reproachfully at him. "It was a simple question, Lana. And a pertinent one, I might add. You're not afraid to answer it, are you?"

"Of course not! I'm a good reporter, Dad.

Maybe . . . maybe I didn't use the best judgment in this case, but I'm a damn good journalist.''

"I know you are." He nodded slowly, thoughtfully. "I never would have encouraged you to take up the profession in the first place if you hadn't been. But I think there are things you've overlooked in your pursuit of a career."

"Such as?"

"Being a good journalist is a big responsibility. It's more than just being able to write. More than gut instinct for a story, or the ability to ferret the truth out of someone. It's also knowing when to back off, when not to push too hard. It's understanding human foibles enough not to injure innocent people. Everybody makes a horse's ass out of himself at some time or another. But that's not necessarily news. There are times when it's better to overlook certain eccentricities or faults in people. And being a good journalist is also admitting when you've made a terrible mistake and taking the necessary steps to redress that wrong."

"I thought that the stories of Abscam and Voz de la Tierra were big news. I never meant to hurt anyone—especially John." Lana stared at her father with pleading eyes. "I never meant to hurt him!"

"Well, I think the first step is to admit that you did hurt him and the cause he has worked so hard for. Once you admit that you were wrong, you can take steps to rectify the damage."

"I don't know how."

"What do you think your first responsibility is?"

"I don't know, I guess...somehow let John know that I was wrong."

"To let John know or the public know?" her father asked pointedly. "I'm talking about responsibility here, not personal feelings."

"You're right," she sighed. "I should let the public know what Voz de la Tierra and its members stand for. But how can I do that? I don't work for any paper any more."

"Neither do I, Lana."

"But I don't have the contacts or the reputation that you have. I can't just walk up to the editor of the *Washington Post* and say, 'Listen, pal, have I got a story for you!'"

Sam leaned back in his seat and smiled. "Why not? Can you give me one good reason why the editor of the *Washington Post* wouldn't buy your article if it was good? Of course not. Newspapers are crying for good stories and it's up to you to provide them with, not just good, but excellent material. You can do it, daughter. But you first have to learn how to pick and choose among the endless variety of subjects out there. Just look around you, Lana, because there are stories to be told. Be selective and find those that will in some way enlighten or encourage or reflect an aspect of this potpourri we call life. And, most of all, you must learn to be kind. Tell the truth, yes. But, be lenient in your condemnation. Be human.''

"It's not the *Washington Post,* but it's a start," Lana decided. The story of Voz de la Tierra and the men who dedicated so much time and money to it was out. This time, she had researched it from every angle and no misconstrued interpretation could be deduced by any reader. The truth was evident. The names of the organization's members were exposed, true; that could not be reversed. But she had spent many hours talking with Dan, learning the facts surrounding the formation of the organization, its purpose, and its ultimate goals, all of which were revealed in her article under the tone of admiration and respect.

She knew that it did not alleviate the damage she had set into motion a month ago, but it did at least help fill in the missing pieces. She also knew that it would not be enough to win back John's trust in her or his love. But she hoped he would at least be able to see that she was now trying. And she had taken great pains to bridge the yawning gap between Dan and her. His friendship had suddenly become very important to her and she fought to gain his respect.

Lana had learned a lot in the last month, about herself and about her life. She hadn't realized before that everyone has to make his own way in life. You have to forge your own path. When things come too easily, as they always had for her, they're not worth much. The only job she'd ever had was the product of her father's intervention. She had never had to work for anything; it had always just been there. Now the easy life was gone. But, strangely enough, it was no great loss.

There was also a sense of freedom in knowing that she could work on whatever she wanted. And this time, she knew what she wanted to do. Without telling her father what she had learned about the first Samuel Munsinger, she had received subliminal encouragement from him to go after it. He had always been the driving force in her life, only now his encouragement had found a way inside of her and she was reacting to her own instincts and judgment.

The morning she drove back up from Denver to Pine Lake Lodge was cool and cloudy. A light rain had been falling for two days and the air had taken on the chill of early fall. Dan had insisted that she stay as his guest at the lodge while she was working on her story about Tin Cup and, as money had suddenly become an important commodity in her life, she jumped at the invitation.

As soon as she checked into her room, she was eager to contact Bessie Calhoun. If she wanted to find out anything more about her great-grandfather's death, Bessie was probably the best person to talk to. Jack Stark and Joshua Pittman had given Lana the location of the old woman's cabin, along with admonitions about the woman's sanity. But Lana was determined to get to the bottom of this. She wanted to know once and for all how and why Samuel Munsinger died. Something deep in the marrow of her bones told her that here was the story she had been waiting all of her life to find. Marketable or not, she sensed that it had to be told.

Dan smoothed his hand lovingly across the map in front of them on the table. "Here is Deadman Gulch, Lana. But there's no way to drive up in there. You can turn off of Spring Creek Road, but Marve will have to park the wagon here, and you'll have to walk the rest of the way."

"Okay." Lana studied the map with intensity. "Stark said it was the only cabin up there, so I don't think I'll have too much trouble finding it."

"Are you sure you don't want me to go with you?"

"I'm sure, Dan. Thanks anyway. Is Marve free to take me this afternoon?"

"Yeah, that's no problem." Dan folded the map up neatly along the creases and handed it to Lana. "Just be careful."

She smiled up at the man who had only recently become one of the best friends she had ever had. "I will, Dan. I promise." She glanced out the window of the dining room, afraid to broach the subject that was foremost in her mind.

Dan did it for her. "John called this morning." He tried to sound casual, but they both knew how full of weight the simple statement was.

Lana jerked her head back toward Dan, but kept her emotions in check. She waited, breathless for any details.

"He's called a press conference for this afternoon to announce his withdrawal from the campaign."

Lana looked down at the floor, trying to hold back the tears that strained for release. "Is it all my fault, Dan? Did I do that much damage to him?"

"No, Lana. I told you the other day, this has been coming on for a long time with him. He's ready for a change. Maybe all the negative publicity lately made it easier for him to make the final decision, but eventually he would have done it anyway."

"Had he—did he say anything about the article? The one on Tierra?"

"Yes, he read it."

"And?"

"He said it was good. 'Beautifully written' was the way he put it, I believe."

Lana sighed heavily, letting out the suspended breath that still harbored so much pain and longing.

"I think he misses you, Lana."

"Then why doesn't he call me? He knows

where I am. Why has he never answered any of the messages I've left for him?"

Dan shrugged philosophically. "Maybe, like you, he just wants to get his life in order first."

Lana frowned. "Or maybe he has no intention of ever contacting me again."

"Maybe," Dan shrugged again, unaware of the painful glint that flashed in Lana's eyes. He knew there was no point in building up her hopes too much. He really didn't know what John would do. He sensed that they were both more in love than either of them realized, but at this stage in John's life, he was as unpredictable as the wind.

The tiny log cabin sat adjacent to the creek, one side of the structure at least a foot lower than the other. The front door was only slightly off level, as if it couldn't decide which side of the house to go with. A thin flume of smoke drifted upward from the stone chimney joining the gray clouds that hung low in the narrow valley.

Lana heard a sharp *thwap* of metal striking stone from the back of the house, so she walked in that direction. As she rounded the corner of the cabin, something smacked her hard in the middle of the chest. Momentarily stunned, she looked down at the slippery, bulging-eyed fish head that lay at her feet.

Another chop brought her eyes up again. Twenty feet away was a tiny woman, dressed in dungarees and a large, faded brown hat, a bloody hatchet gripped tightly in her hand. She glanced up at Lana, pushing the brim of her hat back as she stared with squinting eyes.

Lana swallowed and tried to take her eyes off the hatchet. *Okay, Lana, this is what you get for watching all of those hokey terror movies. Move your feet, girl.* "Hi," she called, smiling cheerily at the stony countenance that greeted her. "Are you Bessie Calhoun?"

"That I am," the old woman answered clearly, never changing her stance or putting the hatchet away.

Lana stood before her, courageously smiling and feeling like an imbecile. "I'm Lana Munsinger. Frederick Munsinger's granddaughter."

The old woman didn't move. "What's that supposed to mean to me?"

Lana was taken aback by the question. Wasn't this the woman whom Frederick once loved? "I...I was under the impression that you... knew him." But then everyone did say she was crazy now, so maybe she just didn't remember. "He was the editor of the paper in—"

"I know who he was. They've been filling you with stories about me, haven't they? Telling you I'm missing a few of my more important marbles. Well, don't you believe it, honey. I live up here by choice. I let 'em think I'm crazy, 'cause that way they won't bother me any more."

"They?" Lana asked, afraid for a moment that they were right about Bessie in Crested Butte and that she really wouldn't get any information out of her.

"The miners," Bessie answered impatiently, leaning over a bucket to lift up another squirming fish. In one swift movement, she smacked its head on the rock, then chopped it off with the sharp blade of her axe. Splitting it lengthwise with a knife she laid on the rock, she tossed the headless, gutted fish into a pail of cold water with a dozen others.

Lana blanched at the entire operation, wishing now she had never come. This was going to be a total waste of time. "Bessie—"

"It's Miss Calhoun, young lady. That's the problem with you younger generation. No respect for your elders. No respect at all."

"Oh, yes. Well, Miss Calhoun, what I was going to say is that the miners have been gone for sixty years."

This time the old lady looked at her as if Lana was the one who was crazy. "That just shows how little you know, young woman." Bessie cackled with giggly laughter. "Just goes to show." She decapitated and sliced another fish before returning her attention to Lana. "I'm not talking about those miners. I'm talking about the new ones."

"What new ones?"

Bessie wiped her hands on her dungarees, then

stuffed her small hands into the front pockets. She looked at Lana with sad, age-lined eyes. "Fred's granddaughter?" she asked softly.

"That's right."

"So what do you want with me? Do the heirs think I've got all of Fred's millions stashed up here somewhere?"

Lana laughed lightly at the woman's sense of humor. They were wrong in Crested Butte. This woman wasn't crazy. She was as sharp as a tack. "No. I'm a writer and I'm doing some research on Tin Cup and my great-grandfather's experiences there. I have reason to believe that he was...well, we were always led to believe that he was killed by Ute Indians, but according to some men in Crested Butte who knew Frederick—"

"Which men?"

"Oh, Jack Stark and Joshua Pittman."

"Stark," she spat. "That gutless old fart. What does he know? Nobody knows anything about it."

"Even you?" Lana asked softly, watching the woman's face closely.

The woman stared back, both of them caught in the stubborn path of each other's eyes. "I know plenty," she finally said. "Go on in the house while I take care of these fish and then we'll talk."

Not wanting to push her luck with the woman, Lana quietly obeyed, but she couldn't help but be curious about what Bessie Calhoun was going to do with all those fish.

The front porch creaked as she stepped onto the wooden platform and she could almost hear the old house groan. She opened the door and stepped into the dark lopsided interior of the cabin. Every square inch of the small, one-room house was filled with furniture and mementos. Faded, lacy curtain material graced the windows and a wooden rack of rifles lined the wall beside the door. An old table with one leg that had been replaced by a tree stump perched in the corner, and an antique pitcher and vase sat atop it. Old black-and-white photographs covered the walls.

There were pictures of young women, dressed in white lace blouses and long gray skirts, children with satin bows and severe Victorian expressions. Along one wall was a beautiful antique desk that would have cost a fortune in a store. And books everywhere. Every shelf, every table, stacked against the walls, and at the end of a tattered Victorian couch were books. Lana picked up one of them. *Paradise Lost.* And another. *Thucydides, The Peloponnesian War.*

She shook her head slowly, marveling as she moved about the room. It was all so contradictory. Ladylike appointments, Greek history books, photographs of Victorian gentility, and a tiny woman who wore dungarees, chopped off the heads of fish, lived in a dilapidated cabin by herself in the mountains, and insisted that she be called Miss Calhoun.

The door creaked and Lana turned as Bessie walked into the cabin. She removed her hat to reveal thin gray hair that was tied in a bun at the back of her head. But the front hair was short and dry and stuck straight out in wild disarray around her face. "Is your grandmother still alive?" she asked, walking over to the window and straightening the rotting lace that hung limply there.

"No, she died when I was a baby. I never knew her."

Bessie looked at Lana, but her eyes were lost in introspective thought. "She was a good woman... but it takes more than that to live up here."

"You knew her?" Lana asked, startled.

"Of course I did. I knew everybody in Crested Butte. That was a long time ago, mind you. Things have changed. New faces, new ideas. Evolution." She sniffed disdainfully.

"Bess—I mean, Miss Calhoun?" Lana puzzled over the questions to ask. "Why are you up here? I mean these books." She pointed to the stacks that lay around the room. "The furniture, the words you use...."

"The term is incongruous," laughed Bessie, delighting in Lana's discomfiture.

"See what I mean?" Lana smiled. "When did you move up here? What did you do before that?"

"Schoolteacher in Crested Butte. First through

eighth grade. That was about as far as anybody went back then.''

"How did you meet my grandfather?"

"I told you, I knew everybody in town." Bessie moved to a hard wooden chair, signaling for Lana to sit on the antique couch, where a puff of dust escaped as she settled herself. "I taught young Sam for a couple of years. I guess he's your father?'' At Lana's nod, she continued. "Your grandmother hated the winters here. And during the Depression, when times were so hard anyway, she just couldn't take it. But Fred was a stubborn man and he refused, cruelly some would say, to go with her back down to the flat.''

"You could hardly call Denver flatland," Lana said.

"Well, it's all relative. And in comparison to Crested Butte, Denver was the flat. Anyway, as the years went by, Fred and I became close friends...more than that, you understand, but friends all the same. When he was fifty-five and ill with cancer, he went home to his wife.''

"Did that bother you...that he went to her in the end?''

"Nah. It was time he went home." Bessie nodded slowly, reaffirming the truth to herself. "It was time.''

"Did Fred ever talk much about his father? About what might have happened in Tin Cup?''

"Only once.''

"What do you mean? He only mentioned his father once?"

"There were people who didn't take kindly to the mention of Samuel Munsinger. Your great-grandfather frightened certain people up on the mountain and that's a dangerous position to be in."

"How did he do that?"

"He found out things about one of the mines outside Tin Cup and he was killed because of it."

"You're sure of that? You're positive it was murder?"

Bessie pushed her tiny frame from the chair and walked over to a large trunk. She bent slowly as if she were in pain, unlocking the latch and opening the lid. Lana watched as she lifted a stack of clothes and books, then pulled an old woolen coat from the bottom. She carried it back over to the chair and sat with it in her lap. Opening the front flap, she reached down into the lining and pulled out several sheets of yellowed paper. She handed them to Lana.

They were dry to the touch and she unfolded them carefully so they wouldn't crumble in her hand. A clipping from a newspaper fell out of the folds and into Lana's lap. She picked it up and stared at the tiny print.

*Rocky Mountain News Service. Friday, August 14, 1881. Reported by Samuel J. Munsinger.*

*Virginia City, Colo.* Though unsuitably high and remote, the entire Taylor Park region is teeming with nearly ten thousand people. Despite the demise of Hillerton, miners continue to stream into the area and now that the gold ore assays out at $1,700 to the ton, the stampede is on. Even the harrowing blast of winter does not deter the parties from purchasing horses, whipsaws, and supplies and packing in with jack mule across the treacherous twelve thousand foot passes. The big money these days is in lode mining, and veins of gold and silver flow like rivers in the womb of the earth up here.

The town of Virginia City has over five hundred houses, many two stories high. Small lots sell for as high as $5,000 and canned goods for a dollar a can. Among the more lucrative and lively business establishments are numerous saloons and dance halls where young ladies, dressed in silk and smelling of cheap perfume, sell dances for from fifty cents to a dollar and sell other assets for considerably more.

These establishments are, of course, kept in their proper perspectives by the churches, schools, newspapers, and even exclusive clubs for the wealthy and prominent men of the community. There are several hotels, including "Aunt Kate" Fisher's and Maggie Loughrey's Pacific where one can pay exorbitant prices for the most unimpressive accommodations.

These miners are a hard breed, and feuds and gun play are common. Bullet holes prominently displayed in the sides of buildings attest to the bad marksmanship of the citizenry.

Houses are built by the townspeople from trees that flourish prolifically in these forests, felled by their own calloused hands after the forty-foot winter snows have melted and after temperatures, sometimes fifty degrees below zero in the dead of winter, have risen to a more congenial degree.

Life, though awe-inspiringly beautiful, is harsh and uncompassionate up this high. But it is full of dauntless, driving hope.

Lana looked up at Bessie and smiled. "Not much economy with words back then."

"No, but newspapers were the major source of information for people, don't forget. And it was the reporter's job not only to report the news but to give the reader a sense of place."

"Well, I certainly don't see anything in this that would make anyone angry." Lana shrugged.

"That's the trouble with people now," Bessie snapped irritably. "No patience. You have to keep reading. The first article was to set the stage for you, give you a feel for the time and what he was writing about. Believe me, you'll notice an abrupt shift in tone in his letter."

Lana folded the article back up carefully and laid it in her lap. Holding the letter up close to her eyes to see the fading ink and decipher the slanted script, she began reading.

November 6, 1881
Avery Hartison
Denver

I've found it, Hartison. It was just as Chipetti's son said. The patent was forgotten. But Chipetti didn't forget and he was killed because of it. By killing him, they thought they had rid themselves of the problem, but they didn't know he had an heir. Not until I told them.

My knowledge has made me many enemies in this godforsaken place and my heart aches with the cold of winter. It is the starving time, the time of disease and death and my news can only bring added burden to these desperate struggling miners and their families. If I do not make it back to civilization, you must nevertheless let the truth be told and let those poor unfortunates who were driven from their land have what they so richly deserve.

Everyone was wrong, my friend. Every-

one. The government, the mining company,
and those who were uprooted because of it.
A wrong has been committed and it is up to
us—or perhaps you—to bring it to light.
Your friend in truth.
Samuel Munsinger

Lana frowned as she folded the letter back up,
placing the clipping carefully between the sheets
of paper. She looked at Bessie in silent bewilderment. What did this mean? What truth needed to
be brought to life? What was worth being killed
over? She thought of the strange epitaph that had
been carved into his tombstone. *I have fought my
battle and lost, but the truth will never die.* What did
it all mean?

"Who was Chipetti?"

"Don't know. Probably some Indian. Though
most of the people up here in the mining camps
hated the Utes, there were a few who befriended
them. It sounds like your great-grandfather was a
friend of this son of Chipetti."

"I just don't understand it," Lana frowned.
"May I keep these?"

"Sure. Fred found those in the lining of that old
coat of Samuel's. I'm actually glad to be getting
them off my hands."

"Did he try to find out what they meant, and
who this Chipetti was?"

"Only once. He mentioned Samuel's death and

the name Chipetti to the head foreman at one of the mines. Wondered if he knew anything about what happened to his father. The foreman didn't, but he obviously mentioned the name to someone who did, because the next day, Fred's house was broken into and most of his furniture was smashed and drawers were emptied. It was a mess. There was also a note that warned Fred to mind his own damn business."

"But surely he didn't stop there! Didn't he even try to follow up on it?"

"Fred wasn't much of an adventurer. He was a simple man, not too bright, not too ambitious. He basically didn't want to get involved."

"And what about you, Miss Calhoun? You knew about all this. Didn't you wonder?"

"A few years after Fred died, I started doing some checking. I knew that it must have to do with one of those mines outside of Tin Cup, but that's all I knew. I went into the college in Gunnison and I checked out every book I could find about the history of the old mining camps up there. Three days later, a vice president of the mining company was lying dead in my front yard . . . and I supposedly shot him in cold blood."

Lana stared at the woman, stunned. "You didn't, did you?"

"No. But it never came to trial. Someone was afraid I knew too much and that if it went to court, I would tell whatever it was they didn't want known. So payoffs were made between powerful men, and from then on I was labeled the crazy woman. See, even if I told all I knew—which was very little—no one would believe me, because I was the crazy woman."

"Is that why you moved up here?"

"Well, I lost my teaching post and there didn't seem much left for me in town. I was too old to do any more fighting, and besides that I was sick and tired of looking at all those spineless coots that lived there. It's better this way."

"You mentioned earlier about the new miners. What did you mean?"

"Amax, Homestake, Ryan Resources, Min-Corp, Dupont—all of that new breed that comes in helicopters and airplanes bringing with them all that sophisticated technology and those fancy legal dance steps. There's a new boom beginning in this mountain kingdom. The same craziness as a hundred years ago. Only the minerals have changed."

"But what would all of this have to do with Tin Cup? Those were gold mines."

"They're reopening some of the mines up there."

"Who is?" Lana asked, feeling a cold chill sliding up her spine. She wasn't sure she even wanted to know.

"I know of two for sure. Ryan Resources and MinCorp."

"Oh, my God," Lana said dully. "What are

they looking for?'' she asked dejectedly, feeling defeated even before she had begun.

"Molybdenum. You going to look into it?"

*Well, here we go again, John. But please don't be involved in this. Please!* Lana looked back at Bessie. "Do I really have any choice?"

## Chapter Eleven

John dropped the backpack onto the ground and began rummaging through it for a fly to fasten to the end of his fishing pole. "I couldn't agree with you more, Jake. But I still think the best defense is going to be in the client's medical problems. We have a lot of precedents for that and I think it will work."

"You may be right," Jake nodded, munching on a pack of sunflower seeds. "I'm just worried as hell about what that guy's going to do on the witness stand."

"I thought we were supposed to be on a vacation," Roger Winthrop complained. "Can't you guys talk about anything but that shyster-run law practice of yours?"

"You're right," John laughed, standing up and slipping the fly on the end of the line. "No more shop talk."

But Jake Mooney frowned and popped another seed into his mouth. "What else is there?" he asked in all seriousness.

Everyone turned toward him and stared down in disbelief until he grinned sheepishly. "Oh... that!"

John stepped to the edge of the creek, which flowed fast and full at this high altitude, and flipped his line into the water. Yes, that. He wasn't sure he even wanted to think about it right now. Not when he was only about twenty miles from the lodge... and from Lana. He raised his eyes to the western mountain ranges, staring hard as if he could actually see the valley that cradled the lodge.

He knew she was there. Dan, trying to sound so casual about it all, had mentioned it the last time they talked. He said she was working on some article about Tin Cup. John thought of the day he and Lana were up there together, standing inside the old lumber mill, his hands against the skin of her back, moving around to touch her breasts.

He expelled a ragged sigh over the direction of his thoughts. At first he had tried not to think about her too much, but soon realized the futility of that. She was permanently ingrained in his every waking and sleeping moment. And maybe she always would be.

He had been tempted so many times to call her, to try and see her, but something always held him back. For the first time in fifteen years, he was getting his life on track and he wasn't sure he wanted anything to derail it again. It had been a difficult decision, but now that he had resigned from the Senate, announcing his retirement from public office and ending any speculation over a try for the presidency or reelection, he felt free and happy for the first time in years. The governor had already appointed someone who was more than acceptable to the Republican party to fill the remaining eleven months of John's term in Congress.

Now John had joined Jake Mooney's law firm in Evergreen. He didn't have that many clients of his own yet, but he realized that it would just take some time for that. He didn't care. For the first time since he had started in the state senate thirteen years ago and then was elected to the U.S. Senate, he had never felt more freedom and satisfaction in his life, and he knew, without a doubt, that he had made the right professional choice.

He had even bought the house he wanted up in the mountains. Everything was working out just the way he had planned and hoped. He shook his head. *No, don't lie to yourself, old buddy. Not everything.* He knew exactly what and who was missing, but he refused to dwell on it too much. He wasn't ready to find out what her true feelings were for him and what those three days at the lodge had meant. If it had all been for the story, he just didn't want to know.

"I've got extra tickets for the Broncos game next week," Roger revealed proudly. "Any of you guys want to go? What do you say, Ryan? John? Hey, Ryan?"

John stared out over the seemingly endless mountain ridges, knowing that eventually he was going to have to get up the nerve to face her and the truth . . . whatever it might be.

*As long as the rivers shall run and the grass shall grow.* Lana pinched the bridge of her nose and closed her eyes tightly, relieving the strain from reading the small print of government treaties for so many hours. She had been sitting in Gunnison's Western State College Library since early morning and, though she had learned much about the history of the area, she still was no closer to the truth.

Only two days ago, she had received the photocopies of the documents she ordered through the Government Printing Office in Washington. Ryan Resources did own a new mine along Willow Creek just outside of Tin Cup. But they were only leasing the land from the government. Further research showed her that seventy-nine per cent of the land in Gunnison County was owned by the federal government, so there was nothing unusual in the leasing transaction. Most of the mines operated that way. And, too, Ryan Resources had certainly not operated any of the mines in 1881 when Samuel Munsinger was killed. Or for that matter when Frederick and Bessie had all their trouble. So what was the problem? There was no problem. Except. . . .

She couldn't stop thinking about what Samuel had said in his letter. *It was just as Chipetti's son said. A wrong has been committed.* Chipetti's son. What wrong? And who the hell was Chipetti?

She returned again to the early history of Gunnison County, looking for any lead among the early settlers here—the Indians. According to treaties signed by the government of the United States, no unauthorized white men would "ever be permitted to pass over, settle upon, or reside in" the territory assigned to the Utes. So, in principle anyway, the Ute Indians controlled the land in Colorado west of the continental divide. But despite the legal restrictions and assurances of the Commissioner of Indian Affairs, the miners continued to trespass onto Ute territory in search of gold and silver.

In 1868, the Indians were pushed back further, and more of their land was taken away. Another treaty was signed and, along with the murky, mystifying language of lawmakers and references to the Great Father and the Great Council in Washington, it stated that "No white person or persons shall be permitted to settle upon or occupy any portion of the territory, or without the consent of the Indians to pass through the same."

But again the miners paid no heed to the treaty. And to top it off, a vilifying, statewide media campaign was waged against the Indians with the slogan being "The Utes Must Go!" Finally at five o'clock in the morning on September 14, 1881, the United States Army gave formal permission for entry onto the old Ute reservation. It was the final clearance. The miners were at last rid of the Utes.

Lana pushed a book aside and picked up another, sighing with fatigue. There was still no explanation for what happened to her great-grandfather or what this had to do with the mines and that terrible wrong that had been committed.

And then something struck a nerve in her memory bank. A twinge of an idea. She flipped through several pages she had been reading in the last book.

In response to a bill passed by Congress in March, 1853, Captain John Gunnison of the Army Topographical Engineers was placed in charge of surveying a central railroad route between the thirty-eighth and thirty-ninth parallels. He was instructed to survey the route through the Rocky Mountains crossing the continental divide.

Gunnison and his large expedition which in-

cluded an artist, an astronomer, and a botanist,
also included an Indian scout whose payment
from the government came in the form of land.
There was nothing more here, so Lana picked up
another book, scanning the index for any refer-
ence to the expedition. Again there was brief
mention. A Ute Indian guide was hired to lead the
party across the precipitous caverns of Lake Fork
and Black Canyon. And finally, in still another
book—a Ute Indian scout agreed to help guide the
party in exchange for a small parcel of land in
the Sawatch Range. The Army captain convinced
the Department of Interior that the payment was
small reward for the services rendered by the Indian. So, agreeing to the Ute's wish for a secret
transaction outside the normal tribal channels, the
government issued a "patent" for the land.

An Indian was hired. Payment in the form of
land. She looked closely at her map, finding Tin
Cup. Bingo! In the Sawatch Range. She unfolded
Samuel's letter and read it again. "The patent was
forgotten. But Chipetti didn't forget." Leaning
back in her chair at the library, Lana smiled. That
was it! It had to be!

It took several days of hard work to find the
information she needed. After hours of searching
through records in the Gunnison Court House,
she learned the section, range, and township of
the area to the west of Tin Cup. Once she had the
legal description, the going became easier. She

traced title to the land back as far as the records in that county went, but everything showed that it was still in the hands of the federal government. There was nothing about any part of it being deeded to a Ute Indian in the mid to late nineteenth century.

Through her father, she got the name of a contact at the Department of Interior in Washington who was willing for some unspecified, future reciprocal favor to spend the time checking the old land records. Two days later, he called her back. And the news was good. In 1853, a small parcel of land in the Sawatch Range was deeded to a man named Niocaaray (Jack) Chipetti.

When the treaty of 1863 and the subsequent treaties of 1868, 1873, and 1880 were signed between the U.S. Government and the Ute Indians, the patent with Chipetti for the small parcel was, quite understandably, overlooked and forgotten in the records of the Department.

So the land belonged to Chipetti all along. But why was he killed over it? Did he try to make a deal with the mining company when they first moved onto his land? Was the price he was asking so exorbitant, or had he threatened to make public his right of ownership to the land where the mine sat and the company representatives simply decided to deal with the Indian in the most expedient way? Perhaps the world would never know. History was full of crimes that had no solution, tales that had no end. Maybe this was one of them.

But, for Lana, what really mattered was that the land belonged to Chipetti, then his son, and perhaps any heirs that he still had. Through the Bureau of Indian Affairs she was able to verify that such was the case. In a small, dusty town 170 miles south of Salt Lake City, a man named John Wilson Chipetti lived with his wife and four children. In the dry, caked front yard of his ramshackle house was a broken air conditioner, two rusted pickup trucks, and a washing machine that had never worked.

The land, where one of the mines was now producing ten thousand tons of molybdenum ore a day, belonged to John Wilson Chipetti. Not to the government. Not to Ryan Resources. Not to MinCorp. It belonged to a Ute Indian whose life had been determined to a major extent by the tragedy of his people in a struggle of greed and power that took place over a hundred years before. For a silent, sullen people driven from their homeland forever into the desolate and barren desert of Utah, this was a triumph. A minor one, but a triumph all the same.

This time, it really was the *Washington Post.* And the *San Francisco Chronicle,* the *Wall Street Journal,* the *Los Angeles Times,* and every major wire service in the country.

At a time when the oil and natural gas prices were soaring, when inflation was once again in the double digits, when large corporations were receiving more and more tax breaks while the middle class individual sank deeper and deeper into the morass of unpaid bills and dwindling savings accounts, a story about one persecuted Indian who triumphed over a corporate giant and whose victory showed that the legal system did truly work for the common man was a media dream-come-true.

And while John Wilson Chipetti was the hero in the story, Lana Munsinger was the gutsy chronicler of this gripping human drama, the new conscience of the people, middle-class America's avenging angel.

She was where she always wanted to be. She was in demand. She was a Munsinger.

"So what's next on the agenda?" Dan asked, leaning back lazily in a deck chair.

Lana gazed out over the valley that was still clinging tenaciously to the yellow glow of fall. "Oh, the wheat farmers' grievance in Kansas. Two farms have already gone up for public auction and the rest of the farmers are screaming about the grain embargo."

"Well, I suppose they have a legitimate beef."

"That," Lana smiled, "is what I'm going to find out."

Dan took a long drink of iced tea and watched

her closely. She had changed a lot in the past couple of months. Matured, developed as a writer and as a professional. But if you looked closely—and he always did—there was a sadness that lurked in the centers of her eyes and at the edge of her smile. It was always there, even in the brighter moments, and he was sure he knew the cause.

"How long will you get to stay with us this time?"

Lana tried to smile, but her mouth turned down at the corners. "I shouldn't even be here now. I have so much to do." She glanced fondly at her friend. "I guess I just need a monthly dose of your presence . . . like a tonic."

"Are you happy, Lana?"

She was quiet for a long pensive moment. "I'm not sure, Dan. I love what I'm doing. I've never realized before that challenge is what life is all about. I love that part of it."

"But?"

"I don't know. I just wish I hadn't made so many mistakes getting to this point in my life."

"Nothing worth having is easy. Which reminds me, John is going to be here tomorrow."

Lana's surprised expression was directed at Dan. "Here? At the lodge?"

"Yes. As you know he had his father buried up here on a piece of land that we—that Voz de la Tierra bought. He had ordered a special engraving for the tombstone and he's bringing it up here to place at the grave."

"Then I must leave today, Dan."

"Why?" He had anticipated her response from the beginning.

"We have talked about this before," Lana snapped, angry at her own futile attempts to forget John. Just the mention of his name was enough to claw at her insides, tearing the fabric of calm control she had worked so hard to construct. "I can't see him, Dan. He doesn't want to see me."

"How do you know that?"

Lana sighed irritably. "He's had plenty of opportunity to call me, to see me if he wanted to. You're only making this harder for me by insisting there is something between us. There isn't. When love is there, it's there. It's not something you sweat and stew about. Not something you have to struggle so hard for."

"Who says?" Dan asked calmly, aware of Lana's increasing agitation.

"Could we please change the subject, Dan?"

"Sure," he replied easily, smiling to himself. "Are you still collecting articles and books on the mining regions?"

"Yes," she breathed deeply, relieved that they were off the topic of John Ryan. "Who knows, maybe someday I'll get it all together in a book. The definitive historical account of the nineteenth century in Colorado." She grinned slightly embarrassed. "Or some such nonsense."

Dan unsnapped the breast pocket on his shirt and reached inside. "Well, the reason I asked was because I found an article the other day that you may not have." He handed it to her and she unfolded it, intrigued with the prospect of more information on the area.

*Crested Butte Pilot News Service. January 10, 1951.*

*Crested Butte.* Willard "Ax-Handle" Johnson, colorful long-time resident of Crested Butte, died yesterday of coronary failure at the age of 91. One of the early settlers to this area, he came by jack mule in 1879 through Cottonwood Pass. He worked the mines in Irwin, Spring Creek City, Hillerton, and Tin Cup. At different times, he also owned a saloon and served a term as mayor of Hillerton.

With his death, an era has ended. Today, that land around Taylor Park is still and silent. The people and their towns are all gone. Wild rose and columbine now grow where houses once stood. A few foundations amidst the grass are all that remain of the dreams of countless men and women.

But, in an interview last year with the *Gunnison News-Champion*, "Ax-Handle" reflected on those days gone by. "We weren't nothing but mortals," he said. "The mountains defeated us, that's all. The mountains and the elements. It's all gone now. The houses, the stores, the churches, the saloons, the voices. Hell, but it don't matter none. We built a life out of what was readily at hand so I guess it weren't much of a loss when it was gone. Never is. I guess ya got to stick it out. Even when you think the vein is run out."

Lana closed her eyes for a minute, then opened them in narrowed accusation on Dan. Her mouth was tight, but slowly, almost imperceptibly, one corner lifted in a wry smile. She shook her head at him. "You are one crafty old son of a gun. Wily as a fox."

Dan feigned his most innocent expression and blank, wide-eyed look.

Lana smiled and expelled a deep breath. "Okay, Dan, what time does John get here tomorrow?"

Sunlight bounced off the deep yellow of aspen trees, a sprightly dance of shimmering light across the lower fringes of the surrounding mountains. Lana walked through the knee-high grass, still damp from the morning dew.

John saw her when she was still a hundred yards away. He had buried the new marker in the ground, the engraved plaque lying flat against the surface of the ground. And now he stood perfectly still, watching her approach, feeling her presence in every muscle of his body. He had wondered when they would see each other again. Had wondered if it would be he or she who would take that first step. He swallowed, aware of the painfully eager electrical impulses inside himself.

Her long, curly hair was whipping about her face and the gold sweater she wore blended perfectly with the aspen trees behind her. As she drew nearer, he noticed the legs of her pants were soaked below the knees.

Lana was aware that John was watching her as she approached and her nerves were twisted in knots of excitement and dread. She felt he could surely hear the singing in them as they cried out in need for his touch.

She finally reached the spot where he was standing and staring at her, but she stayed back about six feet.

"Hello, John."

His gaze dropped to her breasts rising and falling so quickly, then back to her face. "Lana." He made the last few steps himself, closing all but a slim space between them. "How are you?"

"I'm fine," she said, hating every second of this stilted conversation. He was wearing a down vest over a plaid shirt and she longed to reach out and run her hands beneath the layers of material on his chest. "You?"

He glanced over her shoulders toward the hill behind and shrugged. "Okay." He looked at her closely for a long moment, before he said more. "I've heard a lot about you lately. You've done well for yourself."

Lana broke the rigid line of her jaw and smiled. "So have you."

He nodded slowly and expelled a long breath. "Yeah, I have. I'm happy with what I'm doing for the first time in a long, long time."

"Me too. I feel like I'm finally accomplishing something."

"That's great." *We're both happy,* he thought miserably. *Our lives are just the way we want them.* "That's really ... ah ...." The unfinished remark trailed off in the autumn breeze.

"Why did you never return my calls, John?" Lana grit her teeth as she waited for his reply.

*So—* he tightened his jaw, *—the truth is upon us. Well, might as well get it over with.* "I ... wasn't really sure I wanted to hear what you had to say." His eyes shifted nervously around the landscape. "I'm not real big on apologies. People do what they have to do and then move on. I understand that."

"Nobody has to cause another person so much hurt," Lana said dejectedly. "I never meant to hurt you, John. Or—or your father. I tried to stop you before you told him, but—"

"The truth needed to be told. I should have done it a long time ago."

"But it killed him!"

John looked down at Lana and frowned. "The truth didn't kill him, Lana. Cancer did."

"But you told me that it might—when we talked about Abscam, you said there were other lives involved."

John continued frowning as he watched her. "And you thought that— Lana, you didn't think all this time that my father died because I told him what you had written. Did you?"

"I didn't know for sure, John. Dan kept assuring me that it had nothing to do with it but, when you never answered any of my calls or tried to—to see me again, I didn't know what to think."

John shook his head sadly. "I'm sorry, Lana. I had no idea that you thought that or I would have talked to you."

Lana kept her focus steady and her muscles taut so John wouldn't know how deeply his words cut into her. Is that the only reason he would have talked to her? To relieve her of her guilt?

"Why are you doing this to me?" she whispered painfully.

John frowned, puzzled by the question. "Doing what?"

"Making me crawl."

He reached out to place his hands on her shoulders, but stopped at the last minute, letting them fall back to his sides. "I would never make you crawl, Lana. I don't understand what you mean. I told you that you weren't responsible for my father's—"

"I'm not talking about your father!" she snapped, tears beginning to glisten on the lower lids of her eyes. "I'm talking about us! I called you so many times because I couldn't stop thinking about us!"

This time when John's hands lifted to her body they stayed there, his fingers wrapping around the shafts of her upper arms. From where his hands touched her body, tiny neurons of desire arced in his body. "I haven't stopped thinking about us either, Lana. Night and day...you're always on my mind."

"Then why wouldn't you talk to me? Why have you never tried to contact me?"

His eyes swept across her face and neck, lowering to that slim space between them. "I finally have my act together, Lana. I know where I'm going, what I want out of life. I didn't want to know that you had no intention of becoming a part of that. And I didn't want to find out that what happened between us up here was for the story only. I was just avoiding what I thought was the truth."

"You thought I went to bed with you for the story?"

"I thought it was a possibility."

"Well, it wasn't. I went to bed with you because I've never felt like that about another man. Ever. I fell in love with you up here."

John closed his eyes and immediately pulled her against him, enclosing her in the iron-tight circle of his arms. "I guess you should know something about me, Lana. Sometimes I can be really ignorant about the essential things."

She kissed his chest and ran her hands along his back under the down vest. "So I've noticed."

He tilted her face up toward his and smiled. "Sometimes you just have to hit me over the head with a frying pan to get my attention."

"I'll remember that," she said as his face lowered toward hers. One of her hands glided under the vest around to his chest, moving up to wrap around his neck.

"No, remember this." His mouth was gentle at first, opening and closing in a slow building of desire, but the pressure of his lips increased with the intensity of their mutual need for each other. Lana's fingers pulled at the strands of his hair, while his arms closed around her tightly, sealing her within the steel band of his embrace.

His mouth dropped to her throat where he spread kisses from the base of her neck to her ear. "God, I've missed you!"

Lana's eyes smiled into his as he pulled back to look at her, and she relaxed with a slow sigh. "I've missed you too, John."

"Thank you for being the one to take the first step." He kissed her again, long and greedily.

"You're welcome," she said breathlessly. "But I have to confess that Dan deserves some of the credit."

"How's that?"

"When he first told me you were coming up here today, I planned to leave. I was afraid to see you." She smiled at the memory of yesterday. "But Dan, being the old sage that he is, convinced me to stay and at least try."

"To be honest, if I'd known you were here, I might have picked another time to come up here. I guess we owe a lot to Dan."

"Yes, we do." Lana looked toward the grave that still lay under a fresh mound of dirt. "May I see the marker?"

"Of course." John wrapped an arm around her shoulder and led her over to the grave. They were both silent as they read the inscription.

Generations of man have come and gone
exploring these mountains
in search of a dream.
My father has finally reached the top and
here he will dwell and wander with
the wind . . . and the dream will never die.

"Are those your words?" she asked, watching the wistful sadness that moved across his expression.

"Yes."

"It's beautiful, John. It really is."

His gaze lifted over the top of the tombstone to the valley of purple lupine and paintbrush beyond. "Well, he was a beautiful man. He belongs here. I know you and many others think that he only took from the land, but that's not true. He gave a tremendous amount to the people of this state."

"Did you tell him about Tierra? That you were a member?"

"Yes." John smiled and shook his head. "I just wish I'd told him two years ago. It would have saved some anxiety."

"Wasn't he angry?"

"No, he really wasn't." John's own amazement threaded through his words. "He knew I didn't agree with him on everything and he said he even suspected that I might be behind the organization all along."

"Were you upset about what happened up at Tin Cup, about the land belonging to Chipetti?"

"Goodness, no!" John frowned. "Why should I be upset?"

"Well, Ryan Resources did operate that mine."

He shrugged. "That's their problem. And besides, if anybody deserves a break, it's the Indians. Personally, I was overjoyed. The land is such an integral part of their existence, they'll make sure it is not destroyed."

"You're not involving yourself in the family business at all?"

"Nope. I never have, so I see no point in starting now."

"What about Voz de la Tierra? Are you going to continue working with it?"

"Yes. It means a lot to me and I think it has a positive effect on the citizens of this state. By the way, that was a nice piece you wrote about it. I liked it."

"I know," she grinned. "Dan told me."

John shook his head and smiled. "Dan's quite a man." He tightened his grip around her shoulders, pulling her closer to his side. "Come on, I'll show you the next parcel Tierra wants to buy." John took a last loving glance at his father's final resting place before starting out.

They walked across the field and then climbed the rocky hill in front of them. They had to step carefully, helping each other over the lichen-covered boulders, grabbing hold of tree trunks to help them ascend the steep hill. But it was worth all of the work. For when they reached the top, they had an unlimited view of the valleys around them. And though there were still many more ridges much higher than they now were, it felt to Lana as if she were standing at the top of the world.

John stood behind her with his arms wrapped around her waist and he pointed to a valley just to the west. "Right down there. That's what we're bidding on now. Looks like the Garden of Eden, doesn't it?"

Lana smiled. "And here you are up here on Mount Olympus doling it out to the people of Colorado like some benevolent god."

He laughed good-naturedly, lifting the curtain of hair to kiss the side of her neck.

"You really are an extraordinary man, John."

"No, I'm not, Lana. It's just that after all those years of being elected to speak for the people, I decided it was time somebody spoke for the earth."

Lana turned around in his arms to face him. "I still say you're extraordinary, Mr. Ryan."

He looked down at her seriously. "Only to you, lovely lady. But after a few years of living with me, you may change your mind."

She planted her palms on his chest and cocked her head, pursing her lips in speculation. "I certainly hope you're not asking me to live with you *in sin* as they say."

John widened his eyes in a horrified expression. "Why, ma'am, I wouldn't think of besmirching your reputation in such a way."

"Then, exactly what is that you're asking me, kind sir?"

John pulled her over to a soft patch of grass between a stand of fragrant pine trees. "Come down here, darlin'." He lay back in the grass, pulling her on top of him. "Now, you're the investigative reporter, so I'm going to let you figure it out."

"How am I supposed to do that?"

His grin was lopsided and suggestive. "Investigate me," he growled huskily.

"John Ryan, you are a devil in disguise."

He grasped her hips, pulling her tightly between the slight spread of his thighs. He lifted her sweater up, running his cool hands over her back. "You feel so nice."

Lana buried her mouth in his neck and moved one of her hands down the side of his body and onto his thigh. "So do you."

Lifting her higher, he pushed her sweater and bra out of the way and took her breast into his mouth, his tongue rolling back and forth across the tip. "You taste good too," he whispered against her breast, sliding his tongue across her flesh.

Lana slid her hand between their bodies, her fingers working at the snap of his jeans.

"Looking for something?" John laughed huskily against her skin.

"You're incorrigible, John Ryan," she breathed

against his chest. "Yes, I'm on a treasure hunt. Maybe you'd better give me a hand."

"Yeah, maybe in a minute. But your bumbling attempts do more interesting things to me than I think you realize."

"Is that so?" She snaked the zipper down.

A low groan was torn from his throat when she found what she was seeking. "Indubitably so."

Lana's fingers slipped around him and she moved up higher on his body. "I think I won the treasure hunt," she whispered in his ear.

It was several long seconds before John could speak and when he did, his voice was raspy with desire. "People have found a lot of treasures in these mountains. But I found the best one of all in you. Better than gold, or silver. . . .

Lana bit the lobe of his ear. "Or molybbbddde-num. Damn, that's hard to say!"

John laughed urging her tighter against him. "Well, I don't know now. It might be a toss up between you and moly. You're both tough as nails, of course, but I think you're probably a little bit nicer to go to bed with."

"A little bit?" She tightened the grip of her fingers.

John groaned and expelled a deep breath. "Well, I don't want to overly inflate your ego. And if I told you that I would dig for your trea-sures for the rest of our lives, you might think I need you or something."

Lana grinned. "And you don't, of course."

John's mouth moved along her neck beneath her ear, and he rolled over, holding her beneath him. He looked at her for a long, loving moment. "Nah, not a bit."

# Share the joys and sorrows
# of real-life love with
# *Harlequin American Romance!*™

## GET THIS BOOK FREE as your introduction to Harlequin American Romance — an exciting series of romance novels written especially for the American woman of today.

**Mail to:**
**Harlequin Reader Service**

In the U.S.
2504 West Southern Avenue
Tempe, AZ 85282

In Canada
649 Ontario Street
Stratford, Ontario N5A 6W2

**YES!** I want to be one of the first to discover **Harlequin American Romance.** Send me FREE and without obligation *Twice in a Lifetime.* If you do not hear from me after I have examined my FREE book, please send me the 4 new **Harlequin American Romances** each month as soon as they come off the presses. I understand that I will be billed only $2.25 for each book (total $9.00). There are no shipping or handling charges. There is no minimum number of books that I have to purchase. In fact, I may cancel this arrangement at any time. *Twice in a Lifetime* is mine to keep as a FREE gift, even if I do not buy any additional books.

Name _____ (please print)

Address _____ Apt. no. _____

City _____ State/Prov. _____ Zip/Postal Code _____

Signature (If under 18, parent or guardian must sign.)

This offer is limited to one order per household and not valid to current Harlequin American Romance subscribers. We reserve the right to exercise discretion in granting membership. If price changes are necessary, you will be notified.

Offer expires September 30, 1984

154-BPA-NAS4